Praise for *Money to Burn*

'Into the narrow field of Scandinavian multi-decker novels – populated by Jon Fosse and Karl Ove Knausgård – strides a new star ... Buzzes with electricity ... It's intriguing, it's maddening, it's exciting. I'm in'
*Observer*

'Taut and intelligent prose ... there's no doubt about *Money to Burn*: somehow, Nordenhof has managed to write a moving love story and an incendiary indictment of contemporary society'
*Literary Review*

'The start of a new masterpiece of Nordic literature'
*Dag og Tid*

'The most ambitious literary project of the 2020s'
*Jyllands-Posten*

'Crackles with indignation, conviction, ferocious wit and savvy human insight. Startling, irresistible and thoroughly enlivening, reading her words is not unlike looking at the entrancing flames of a tremendous fire'
Claire-Louise Bennett, author of *Checkout 19*

'Unusual, fascinating and complicated in the best way'
Claire Fuller, author of *Unsettled Ground*

'A comet in Scandinavian literature. Her sentences are like lightning: they hold great beauty and destruction. Funny, furious and masterful – *Money to Burn* is a declaration of war against capitalism'
Olga Ravn, author of *My Work*

'What blew me away was how – with its shard-like chapters – *Money to Burn* renders not only the inner lives of the married couple at the centre of the story with truth and depth, but something of the texture of their individual existence, their ways of being in the world, together and apart. Nordenhof's writing is electrifying'
Chetna Maroo, author of *Western Lane*

'Direct and full of fervour. I loved how fast it makes its moves and how much grandeur it achieves. I need the next instalment desperately'
Adam Thirlwell, author of *The Future Future*

'Entirely intoxicating and compulsive, this is a story in the hands of an utterly remarkable writer, and has me very much desperate to read more. Perfect'
Ore Agbaje-Williams, author of *The Three of Us*

## ASTA OLIVIA NORDENHOF

Asta Olivia Nordenhof is an award-winning poet and author. *Money to Burn*, the first book in the Scandinavian Star septology, was first published in Denmark in 2020. It was awarded the PO Enquist Prize and the European Union Prize for Literature and was shortlisted for the Nordic Council Literature Prize. An international sensation and translated into eighteen languages, *Money to Burn* was published in English by Jonathan Cape. *The Devil Book* is the second in the series and was an instant bestseller upon first publication in Denmark.

## CAROLINE WAIGHT

Caroline Waight is an award-winning literary translator working from Danish, German and Norwegian. Her translations include books by Caroline Albertine Minor, Ingvild Rishøi, Maren Uthaug and Dorthe Nors. She was a finalist for the 2023 PEN Translation Award and received a special commendation at the 2023 Warwick Prize for Women in Translation.

ASTA OLIVIA NORDENHOF

# Money to Burn

TRANSLATED FROM THE DANISH BY
Caroline Waight

VINTAGE

3 5 7 9 10 8 6 4

Vintage is part of the Penguin Random House group of companies

Vintage, Penguin Random House UK, One Embassy Gardens,
8 Viaduct Gardens, London SW11 7BW

penguin.co.uk/vintage
global.penguinrandomhouse.com

First published in Vintage in 2026
First published in hardback in Great Britain with the title
*Money to Burn* by Jonathan Cape in 2025
First published in Denmark with the title *Penge på
lommen* by Forlaget Basilisk, Denmark in 2020

Copyright © Asta Olivia Nordenhof 2020
Translation copyright © Caroline Waight 2025

The moral right of the copyright holders has been asserted

Penguin Random House values and supports copyright.
Copyright fuels creativity, encourages diverse voices, promotes freedom
of expression and supports a vibrant culture. Thank you for purchasing
an authorised edition of this book and for respecting intellectual property
laws by not reproducing, scanning or distributing any part of it by any
means without permission. You are supporting authors and enabling
Penguin Random House to continue to publish books for everyone.
No part of this book may be used or reproduced in any manner for the
purpose of training artificial intelligence technologies or systems.
In accordance with Article 4(3) of the DSM Directive 2019/790,
Penguin Random House expressly reserves this work from the
text and data mining exception.

Printed and bound in Great Britain by Clays Ltd, Elcograf S.p.A.

The authorised representative in the EEA is Penguin Random House
Ireland, Morrison Chambers, 32 Nassau Street, Dublin D02 YH68

A CIP catalogue record for this book is available from the British Library

ISBN 9781529934533

Penguin Random House is committed to a sustainable future
for our business, our readers and our planet. This book is made
from Forest Stewardship Council® certified paper.

# DREAMFACE

I was on Funen, headed somewhere on a bus. It pulled over at the roadside, and when it did a white-haired man outside was looking in at me. I can't explain why – he looked like so many other men – but when the bus set off again I had the eerie sense that I was carrying some part of him with me. For a while after that, I found it increasingly difficult to concentrate on anything else. I couldn't help it. I was trying to recall his face. It felt like something from a dream, quite clear in front of me, and yet I couldn't pick out a single detail. Out of the dreamface came the inkling of a farm, three buildings around a yard, and I pictured its walls, sleek and still at night. I would have liked to forget him, but he kept quivering strangely at my back. I was being pursued, but it was more than that – my pursuer had stepped inside me and was peering back out at himself. This went on for several weeks, until I realised that I had to go back to the place where I'd first seen him.

From Nyborg Station I walked down the deserted street into town. I bought a beer at a pizzeria and found a seat overlooking the castle to drink it. It was hot. Only a few people out. They went around in little clusters, and in little clusters they sat down with ice-cream cones. The low water in the moat was very still, still enough to see it set in motion by a dragonfly. A huddle of ducklings sat on a rock warmed by the sun. Then I picked myself up, and went off to find the bus I'd taken.

Not that I saw him again, of course. I went all the way to the final stop. The driver twisted around towards the empty rows of seats, and when he realised I was planning to ride the whole way back to Nyborg, he said I knew how to make the most of a sunny day. We were nearly back in town when suddenly I flailed my arm and asked him to stop. I'd seen a farm; I was getting off.

In the yard I rang the bell. No answer. *Anne-Mette, Henrik, Emma and Lukas* read the door plate, but none of those names sat right with what was quivering inside me, making me afraid. How could I be sure this was the farmhouse from my visions? I sat down on a bench and closed my eyes. Then things started coming back to me. Over there, that must have been the barn. It's been torn down since. And over there the horse: Turner. Kurt, that was his name, I think he was the one in charge, but relatively late in life, because he never really took to the role: it rested, shrill and threatening, on his surface. Two employees, Lars and Fatih. At night the walls are still and sleek, mosquitos swarming, buses in the barn. Kurt's Bus Company, his plain-named business. At night the buses are in the barn, and someone lies awake in bed. It's Maggie.

# KURT

It's late morning. Kurt is alone in his office. It's hot. On the wall is a calendar distributed by an expensive brand of underwear. Maggie picked it up at some shop. She wasn't sure what else to do with it but pass it on to Kurt, and he wasn't sure what to do with it but pin it up. He doesn't understand the pictures, they seem cold to him, and he gets confused wondering what Maggie thinks he thinks of them. Was she genuinely trying to please him, or was it merely a way of seeming generous? Should he take it as contemptuous and be offended? Should he have refused the gift? Was it meant to be a question, and if so, what was the question? He forgets to change the month, leaves January up well into May, then fumbles through to the right woman, hurried and distracted. But if anybody walked in, he'd be ready. He'd turn and say he wasn't sure what he was doing, really, but he's innocent. He's not the one to blame here.

The phone rings, and he explains for the fourth time to a certain Henrik Mikkelsen that no, he doesn't need to pay until he boards the bus and yes, of course he can reserve the seats up front. Kurt is always wary of the telephone. When it rings it feels like wire along his spine, and when it doesn't, he is waiting. He speaks very loudly into the receiver, standing up and pacing in the tiny semicircle permitted by the cord; he nearly yanks the phone off the edge of the desk and scrabbles it back into place. He has got into the habit of tapping on the desk with the flat of his hand after he hangs up – it's his way of being sure the call took place. It's so easy to lose your bearings, to mix up names and dates. Sometimes, after a conversation, it dawns on him he can't recall a word of what was said. Then he has to call back, apologise profusely, say he spilled a cup of coffee on the bits of paper. Or – if the name and number of the caller have entirely slipped his mind – he simply has to hope it'll all work out.

Now he's gone out to the barn. It's a large space, and he has walked all the way through it to the far wall, where the straw is stacked in bales. It was bought for Turner, but then suddenly she died. Suddenly, thinks Kurt, even though Turner was old and her coat was flecked with grey, even though he never rode her any more but put the bridle on and led her past the fields and into the woods. He told Maggie he was still riding. He couldn't bear to admit Turner's frailty. He kept her old age a secret, even to himself – or rather, he split himself in two: the Kurt who knew to lead and stroke his ageing horse and say goodbye, and the Kurt who didn't know, or had forgotten what it meant.

He feels solemnity in here. In the winter especially, when the cold in the barn is greater and more sonorous than outside, but even now, in this warm and stagnant air. In here he can shrug off Maggie's disapproval, because he's done something he didn't think he was capable of. He has persisted. Before they came to Nyborg, there was only drifting. He was barely a man at all. He had nothing but his hands, and those weren't good for much. He could fall in love with almost anyone: Maggie, in the end, the last in a very long line. He lived his life at night, meeting new friends who dreamed of fast cash and affection, of doing something with their lives, but never what they'd been offered. Never in the same bed twice. Yet the enthusiasms of the night before always seemed trickier in the morning – where to start? – and he would go home in a thin, already pale euphoria. Once home, misgivings: am I loved, or am I a pariah? So he had to set back out again the next night. His wife at the time, Ulla, she'd put up with it. She didn't think another man would be much different, and was nervous of replacing Kurt with someone who spent more time at home. She loved the hours alone at night, and the bed, which was large and peaceful without a man in it. Ulla had made her calculations, and although he drank a large part of his inconsistent income, she was still better off married than divorced. In any case, she liked that the fridge was always stocked with beer. When Maggie came into the picture, it was more the fear of being left broke than any sense of honour or the insult of the younger woman's body that made her throw a rye-bread sandwich at Kurt's head. He stood slack-jawed, until suddenly he turned angry and starting yelling, said that it was her fault he was like this.

Kurt sits on a crate. He fills his lungs with warm air, holds it, lets it go. This is an important time of day. Doing his rounds in the barn. This is where he is reminded he has lived, he has held something in his hands. I haven't sunk that low. Not *that* low. He comes to this conclusion every day. He must snatch it somehow from the flames, carry it the way you carry an innocent child, away, to some safe distance from the fire. Then he can have his two minutes of peace.

He thinks about the money in his bank account, and reverts into his fearful, frantic self. The business has been doing well for three years running, he's saved quite a bit, and now that he's thinking of investing it the prospect is almost painful. He has to be careful about what he chooses. He doesn't want to invest in the past – he dreams of something altogether new.

The yard is thick and still with sunlight. Kurt stops short. For a moment his mind is also still, it is a single sunny wasteland, then with a sloshing sound it kicks back into gear again. He hurries towards the office, and once inside he circles a bit before flopping down into his chair. As a rule he is in the office or he is out. Only late at night, when he's tired enough to fall asleep immediately, does he go trudging through the main house and into the bedroom.

Yesterday, against his usual routine, he decided to spend the evening at home with Maggie. It was obvious she wasn't happy about it. She sat very stiffly on the sofa, darting him the occasional sidelong glance, the way a heron does, without moving another muscle of her body. He wanted to say something, bind them together in the space, but before he could think of so much as a word Maggie had soaked it up into herself and into her silence.

There is a quivering around the telephone. Kurt's vision swims. It's as though everything contained and held in place by the ring binders on the shelf, the annual accounts, the lists of customers, has been set into motion and is skidding away.

When he used to write in his notebook at school, he would keep an eye on the words to make sure they stayed where they were put. If he didn't keep a close eye, they might start writing what was actually on his mind. One day the teacher took the notebook home over the weekend, and he lay awake worrying about what she'd find in it. He fell asleep, and woke up with the sense that she'd been watching over his bed all night long. It was then he began to worry about his face, what his face was writing for the grown-ups to read while he slept.

The day has got away from him. He's made phone calls, checked names off a list on the desk, and yet he can't quite put his finger on it – what has he been doing, and what is there still left to do? He stares out at the apple tree, as though it might tell him what his job entails. He does know he has to go to the bank today. He can't put that off any longer.

He does a quick loop around the yard, hoping to find Lars in the workshop so he can tell him all the things he hates about the bank. There's the chitchat among the staff, for one thing, and the way they suck their words inwards as he enters and walks up to the desk, drawing them back into heads that swell like balloons. It's so silent standing there that he can hear the dust moving in the air. Then there's the hideous carpet, which puts Kurt in mind of damp rye bread.

Once, when they both happened to be at the garage at the same time, his adviser from the bank cracked a joke about old folk still hiding money at home. I'll do what I want with my money, Kurt thought. He'd been halfway through slitting a hole in the mattress when Maggie appeared in the doorframe, scowling at him in a way that drew his gaze out of himself and into her, and suddenly he could see what he looked like, standing there with the knife raised like a madman. All that he could think to do was stay completely still. Maggie turned away, but a few steps down the corridor she turned to him again and spoke: You can sew that back up yourself.

Kurt could picture it vividly: Maggie taking out the money, Maggie throwing it into the hearth to punish him for the thing he doesn't understand (but understands he's always being accused of), so he sewed the mattress back up and hid it elsewhere. Over the next few months, he kept checking for signs that she'd tried to reopen the mattress. He thinks it's cold of her, unloving, that she didn't want to know *how* much money he *would* have sewn in.

The bank went alright. He was only there to cash a cheque, but he doesn't understand why he always feels as though he's being taken to task. He's the one who's built a business from the ground up, he's the one making a profit, and yet somehow he feels inferior to this high-street lot with their budgeting advice and earnest faces.

He hangs up the phone. That was Bent, asking if Kurt wanted to go out later. For a minute Kurt was hoping he meant just the two of them, but of course he meant the Russian too. The Russian – Yugoslavian, actually, but everybody thinks he's Russian – materialised in Nyborg last summer out of thin air, and suddenly he was everywhere, acting like his presence wasn't surprising. His name is Jovan, and he instantly awoke in Kurt an urge for violence, which Kurt is now waiting fretfully for him to vindicate.

One episode in particular he can't shake off. A night out, and afterwards a few of them went back to Jovan's place to carry on drinking. It was late. The mood was fuddled, overcooked. The booze ran out, the high deflating slowly. Dawn broke. Ghita and Lene were there, Bent and his cousin.

There came a point where nobody had spoken for ages. It was time, really, for them to go their separate ways, but each was hoping that none of them would break the spell, that no one would transform the night – which had been good to them – into a long and lonely day. Suddenly, Jovan emerged from the kitchen, stuck a bunch of herbs under Kurt's nose and said, *Smell this*. A fierce tingle ran from nose to forehead. Kurt leapt up, arms flailing wildly. It felt like ants were inside his head. Something dislodged in the group: they laughed and laughed, and every time the laughter died away, someone started up again and shook it loose in all the others, engulfing them in a vast and happy scorn. Kurt's distress, Kurt's little comedy was just what they needed, and suddenly there wasn't anything they wouldn't laugh at. He was crushed. He wanted to leave, but he knew that if he did his defeat would be all the more absolute. There was nothing for it but to let the laughter roll on over him, its insignificant object.

And now, if he wants to drink with Bent, he has to stomach drinking with Jovan. The two have joined forces on a few projects. That's as much as Kurt's allowed to know, and he's revolted by Bent's new leather jacket and the smug smile that came with the jacket and the new projects.

Bent's face beside the record player is the consistency of porridge. Kurt stops bothering to focus – it makes him nauseous when he tries. He reaches for his beer, and his hand is like a sluggish swarm of bees. He can sense Lene sidling closer and remembers the aroma of toasted buttermilk buns wafting in from the kitchen the last time he spent the night at hers, a homey scent that suddenly distorted things and made him feel disgusted by her. The kitchen stool felt absurdly small beneath him as he tried to choke down a piece of the dry roll. He could already feel Sofie's derisory stare from the kitchen window on his return home, as he slouched across the yard and made straight for his office.

Sofie, his overgrown child. When she was still living with them, he'd see her sitting in the kitchen with Maggie and think, *When, when* will she move out? But now that she finally has, he doesn't know what life is any more. Now and then he opens the door to her old bedroom and the loss strikes him anew, like opening the door to a sauna, making him gasp for breath and shut the door again.

\*

HOW ABOUT QUEEN? Bent shouts from over by the sound system. Lene laughs. She looks like dough left to rise too long. A vague aversion – or is this what they call desire? – is buzzing in Kurt's forehead. With a rage as flat as a sofa-squashed fart, he watches Jovan and Marie get up and thrash around to a song that is apparently about bicycles. It feels like being locked inside a thermos. Like shrieking from inside a sealed compartment, but outside all you hear is a faint squeak. Lene, he says cajolingly, his face very close to hers, I feel like I'm inside a thermos. She looks at him, distracted, laughs her doughy laugh again, and Kurt, he thinks it's funny too, he's come up with a good one. Suddenly, he's in a better mood.

HEY BENT BENT

WHY DON'T WE GO TO

THE PHOENIX?

he shouts.

It is night, but thin night, nearly morning, when somehow Kurt – he will forget how, so we must observe him – makes his way home through the town, past houses and into the periphery of Nyborg, where the farm is, the buses, the barn, Maggie, the emptiness that Sofie gave him when she moved out, where everything is that is his.

It is by an effort of the heart, by some unutterable knowledge of where he belongs, that he finds his bed, and with a sluggish awareness that he is Kurt, though the notion is heavy as blood, he falls into the noisy sleep that wakes Maggie.

# MAGGIE WAKES

Are you awake, Maggie? I've been wanting you. Tell me something.

I think your husband woke you with his snoring. You can smell the pub on him, but maybe something else is on your mind?

Maggie sits up in bed. She gives Kurt a brief and bitter glance, then that's done with. She feels but doesn't see the apple tree in bloom behind her back, the sun already baking on the felt roof. There's a saying: I feel like the yolk in an egg. It's supposed to be a good thing.

Maggie doesn't know what morning is, now that morning isn't waiting for Sofie to wake up, for Sofie to make it so she doesn't have to think of things to do. She puts the water on for coffee, everything inside her pulling left, towards where Sofie's room still is, although it's empty of the items that mattered enough for Sofie to take them with her. It hurts to think of the bedside table, which Maggie painted Sofie's three favourite colours, blue, red and yellow, and gave her as a present for her eighteenth birthday. That's still in there.

She can't really fault her for leaving it, though she's tried. She's gone all the way back to the pain of childbirth trying to find a point where she can tap into the rage, but she keeps coming up against that piece of furniture, the unlovely product of her hopes, and there she always stops. Even so, it hurts to think about the bedside table, in the silence of Sofie's room. The drawer is empty, she's checked. She had to know if it was empty, or if it still contained something. She dreams them up, the objects Sofie might have put in there. Leather bracelets, important letters. Memories, amulets no one else can understand: an empty pack of cigarettes from a particular evening, a boiled sweet melted into a paper bag.

The kettle boils and whistles. Maggie pictures Kurt in there, whistling to be let out, and can't help but smile.

There's a question inside her – does she love Kurt? – that has long since ceased to be a question, and is now its own cell, dividing and dividing but never truly splitting apart. She files it under *stupid thoughts*. Long ago, back when she was always short of cash, she thought constantly of all the things the small amount of money she had then could have bought her a hundred years before. Another example of a *stupid thought*.

She sits down with her coffee and leafs through the newspaper. Miners are striking in England. Thatcher has announced she'll put a stop to it. Strikes and demonstrations in Poland. She stares for a while at a picture of a man holding up a sign, which the caption says reads *bread and freedom*. She's fascinated by his face. There is a calm to it she assumes must be because the words *bread and freedom* capture everything he wants to say. For a moment she sees the kitchen through the certainty of the man's words, and the kitchen takes a turn towards the strange – it almost seems to tilt.

There's an article about the new national TV channel. There's going to be more local programming, it says. If there's one thing Maggie doesn't want to know any more about, it's Funen. Kurt told her once that when he was young he'd gone out with a nice girl from the village. Sometimes those words – a nice girl from the village – light up inside her like a neon sign, and she almost can't get past it.

The boyfriends she had before Kurt are arrayed in her mind's eye like a series of peculiar questions. More questions, but what are they asking?

There was the one who dropped the plum he was eating, and looked like an ape as he went chasing after the fruit rolling through the living room, arms outstretched in front of him. There was the one who'd sat beside her on a bench, his eyes beautiful and sad. She'd gone out with someone else while he was in Paris, so she'd had to refuse the gift he'd brought back for her. I don't want to give this to you now, he'd said, and that was the first time she had realised he'd been serious about her.

No, she's not suited to living with a man. The morning grows ever more saturated with sunshine, and everything she does, she does in the vague fear that Kurt might wake, might come to her and knock her off course.

Maggie turns over the spoon to make sure she's rinsed off all the porridge, but forgets the point of what she's doing. She gets lost in the shiny thing, hoping that eventually the spoon itself will jog her out of her reverie. Then she shakes her head vehemently, puts the spoon back under the tap. All around the house there are stubble fields. There is a single low tree here and there along the edges of them, but otherwise all is level and machine-cut. Maggie thinks about the asylums, if they're still called that, about lives gone wrong and penned inside square-walled rooms, and she looks out at the countryside, which is carved up into squares, and soon she can't tell the difference between inside and out.

The other day, by accident – well, by design – she took a magazine from the hairdresser's. She had neglected her hair for several years, letting it grow dry and wispy, increasingly dreading the moment when she'd have to meet the stylist's eye in the mirror. Sitting in the salon chair, noticing with sudden clarity her ragged cuticles, she tried to hide as many fingers as possible under the magazine. She withdrew into the simple-mindedness that seemed necessary in order to justify her lack of grooming, letting her eyes wander and agreeing to any idea the hairdresser threw out – it was all the same to her, volume, length – and since she'd already made herself look like an idiot, she thought she might as well stuff the magazine into her bag. It would be easy to claim she simply didn't understand you weren't allowed. Back at home she sat down and read furiously about which hats were in that season, and with every hat she read about, the rage narrowed and came to a point.

In a way it was easier when Sofie was little and Maggie always had her hands full, and passed out the minute her head hit the pillow in the evening. Now all these dreams she has time to dream are making her grotesque. She can picture a room filled solely with hats, vast long shelves of hats in red velour and hats meant to sit at an angle, long elegant cigarettes and decorative flowers that open almost like a dragon's maw at the foot of a broad flight of stairs, red and orange flowers gushing in her direction. She can picture a very different woman, the woman she might have been if things had not gone quite like this, and this woman is still very beautiful, and not trampled on by life, like she is, and this woman is above all calm and in no rush to answer, she plucks her words as though from softest water, lowers her rope and draws up the words that have stayed with her, and they are simple words: bike, gooseflesh, jetty.

The worst fantasies are the ones about how little it would have taken for everything to be completely different. A hesitation one night, some sudden but insignificant occurrence that led her in another direction, and not ultimately into the arms of this life, which she believes began with Kurt.

\*

What is there to do? She could search far back into her past. Very gingerly, trying to delay them, she shapes her mouth around the words. They pour out of her too quickly otherwise. What emerges is her first memory:

Her hair is braided. Everyone surrounds her in a circle, adults and most likely children too, but the children she pays no attention, it's the sea of grown-up faces, broken with emotion, that have stayed with her all her life, hot and cloudy. She doesn't actually know how long they were in the bunker, she doesn't have anyone to ask. But it feels like she entertained the circle for hours. She played all the parts, horse, dog and rider, startling herself and rearing up when the dog bit the horse's leg, then bursting into song. By now she understands, of course, that the grown-ups' devotion was a devotion to life itself, to the child as child, that she was always going to feel betrayed when the siren stopped and the faces turned away from her again. But even then, she also knew she'd created an artist, that it takes a special kind of child to earn the love of adults. Not long after that the war was over, making this her only memory of it. The rest she had to teach herself as time went on, in slow drags or in jolts, absorbing and rejecting.

The drawer sticks, calling her back to the present. She's asked Kurt to fix it countless times, but he can't muster an interest in anything that's not mechanical, and it doesn't occur to Maggie to try to do it herself. She accepts that she will stand here every day and wrestle with the drawer, adding this, too, to the silent case she's building against Kurt.

She lifts the receiver off the wall, presses the first few digits, then thinks twice. Plans ahead, tries to formulate the sentence that will justify the call. I just wanted to ask how you're getting on in Odense, she hears herself say, and cringes. She feels like she's been snipped out of a catalogue. Like somebody has written over her love, making it abruptly stiff and stupid.

She saw a dead duck when she was cycling home from the supermarket. It was lying on the gravel track that leads to the house, and it wasn't there – or so she thinks – when she left. She can't understand it. There's no water near by, there aren't normally any ducks. Most of all she couldn't understand why it was dead. It's hard to accept. She was confused. She stayed rigid and still, watching to make sure the smooth round breast wasn't moving. No, it hit her with a jolt as she continued home with her back to the dead bird, it definitely wasn't moving, and she pedalled more quickly than usual.

She lifts the receiver off the wall again, dials the whole number and waits on tenterhooks. Oh hello, it's Mum, I just saw a dead duck, she begins.

Fatih and Lars are in the yard, sorting through spare parts and tools. Maggie watches from the window as they work, surrounded by objects and containers. She knows, because Kurt has told her, that he only employs people like himself, who know not only how to drive a bus but also what it's made of. But the knowledge these men have she can't even begin to understand. It turns into a jumble of component parts. The mere thought of all those tiny pieces is disconcerting, and it seems to her – if she opens her mind even a little to the idea that you can take a bus apart – that it's madness it was ever whole at all, and trundling down a country road. She begrudges Kurt the gaze that picks things apart. The stove that was once hers and not up for discussion is suddenly a collection of heating elements and wires that can be coupled and uncoupled, and she doesn't even want to think about the coffee machine, what leads to what and where; no, the filling of the jug is the magical result of agreements best left undisturbed. Either it works or it doesn't, Maggie declares, with the fatalism which, if she lets go, well – how could she go on?

She draws back from the window, takes a seat in the armchair and tries to resettle her mind. One thing at a time, she reminds herself, and she searches, eyes wandering, for an object in the living room to focus on as the one thing. But everything bleeds into everything else – she's barely started thinking about watering the potted plants when she might as well plump up the sofa cushions or finally get around to storing away her winter coat. *This is my life, then,* she thinks, the words captioning the moment, and with a fine sense of theatre she sees her life reflected back to her in a garbled, clownish version.

She sits for a while, then on a sudden impulse she returns to the window and watches the men. Fatih holds up an object, exchanges a few words with Lars, and places it in the container appropriate to the conclusion they've reached. She sees, she takes it in, but she wouldn't be able to recount what she's seen. To her, the two of them are merely fainter expressions of Kurt; they're part of what he carries around with him. Just as she, to them, is merely the backdrop Kurt emerges from, giving him a resonance he wouldn't otherwise have had.

An idea – tiny, swift and hard, like a nut falling from a tree – comes whistling down through Maggie and lands in her lap: she was young, once.

# EVENTS IN MAGGIE'S YOUTH

I want to be happy on the first page of this chapter, Maggie says.

I want to be going home alone with a Coke.

It's a little after midnight, and if you opened up my heart, it would say nothing but *Coke*.

Maggie is evaluating her belongings. She lays out all her jumpers and considers each one carefully before neatly folding them again and returning them to the wardrobe.

There is a black jumper with batwing sleeves she loves. She can sense it in the wardrobe as she stares at the closed door.

She looks at the covers of the five records she owns. They're from Brazil – she was given them by a guy whose mother was Brazilian. She hasn't listened to them because she doesn't have a record player. On one cover there's an outsized tiger, and a golden flight of stairs that leads into its belly. She props the records up against the wall, putting the one with the tiger at the front. She imagines having visitors, people wondering about the records, and she looks forward to saying they're from Brazil.

After that she isn't sure what else to do. She eats a tin of sweetcorn, feeling out of place in the small half-empty council bedsit.

*

On the first of every month, she goes down to an office and is handed an envelope containing what seems to her a fortune. On those days she forgets entirely what it's like to queue at the grocer's, to count on her fingers if she has enough for bread as well as milk, and she goes out and buys blouses and lacy knickers.

After a sleepless night she unfolds a few bills at the ticket desk. *Next train to Rome, please.* There's a brief moment of horror when, at the station in Basel, she accidentally spends the last of her cash on a slice of tart, but she admonishes herself: a beautiful young woman can always find money and food if she's willing to do what it takes.

Then the train pulls in at Termini, and there's a vast impression of orange, which she carries with her into the arrivals hall. In the heaving crowd she feels that life is very easy: all she needs to do is set out, go into the streets. At the first four hotels the staff are altogether too professional, but at the fifth she senses instantly the clerk can be seduced.

She promises she'll have the money in the morning. Her old Nonna, she says, or tries to say in broken English, didn't meet her at the station as agreed, her beloved Nonna whom she hasn't seen since childhood, and she's getting worried now, because Nonna's health is failing, she might have fallen; oh yes, she's tried calling, even gone round to the flat, but no one answered the door, it's terrible, but most likely – right, yes, she's a bit senile too – most likely she's just dozed off and forgotten it was meant to be today, but at any rate she'll definitely have the money tomorrow, she promises, conscious all the time of her short skirt.

For a day or two she carries on like that, then she has to move on. It's almost as though it isn't her, only a laugh that slips out through the foyer and sets off running down the street. On the broad steps outside a church she sits down to consider her next move. No more hotels – she doesn't want to push her luck.

Going into the park, she finds a dog and strokes its sun-slicked head, and it follows her around for the rest of the day. You stay here now, she says to it in Danish when she leaves the park that night. No, sit. Stay. In the end she says it much too angrily, and she can still feel the skinny dog's eyes on her as she takes a seat at a bar and orders beer and peanuts, but she forgets about it when a nearby group of people wave her over. A man, quite good-looking, pulls out a chair, and she says *grazie* – she's been practising since home. It's almost unbearably cinematic, the way he guides her to his flat through broad streets, one arm around her shoulders.

The days are the best. He's out, he's at work. She doesn't really care enough to try to get to the bottom of what he does. He works at a ministry, she does know that, and she's happy not speaking English or Italian well enough to understand more. They like listening to each other talk, but they can't really hear each other. Language has already failed them. They have no option but complete indulgence.

*

Yes, she loves those days. Long mornings behind shuttered windowpanes, heavy wooden furniture. She arranges everything at her bedside: grapes, a glass of water, paper to write on. She woke up with a tune in her head, and now she wants to find the lyrics for it. But then the bed won't do; she starts again at the kitchen table or in the uncomfortable reading chair and gives up, absent-minded, unperturbed, to investigate instead the contents of his cabinets and drawers. There is silverware in elegant boxes. And shirts, endless shirts, purple, lime and blue-striped, cypress. She takes the feeling of all those shirts when she goes out onto the balcony. A woman carrying lots of little bags is trying to call over her child, who has stopped outside a greengrocer's, thrilling over all the fruit. Maggie rests her cheek against the balustrade, still saturated with the cool of night, and thinks of all the films she's ever seen. The girl on the balcony – it could be a title – and now she can't wait for the next scene, the one where he comes home and lifts her up onto the kitchen counter.

No more men, they're pigs. Female friends, she promises herself, and when she's back in Copenhagen she puts an advert in the newspaper to say she's looking for a pen pal. She starts a correspondence with a girl in Slangerup, Christina – a long series of superficial letters on topics she deems suitable. She writes about guitarists and dresses, and although she's interested in those things, she genuinely is, she tries so hard to sound a certain way that everything she loves vanishes on the paper. She spends hours, discards countless drafts, until eventually she has a letter that sounds more or less identical to the last one Christina sent her.

One day she goes to Slangerup, but she doesn't know how to behave on a weekend visit. She stands stiffly behind her chair as the plate of chicken is carried to the table, and she can see Christina's father trying to compress his lips around a laugh as he invites her to sit down. How is Maggie supposed to know what a family is like? She feels humiliated and too tall among these people, who are all short, and would have rushed straight back to the station if she wasn't pinned in place by shame. I live in Copenhagen, here and there, she says in answer to Christina's mother, and although the mother's face is craven now, she'll be cracking jokes about her daughter's Copenhagen friend as soon as she's out the door. If you opened my heart with a knife, she thinks on the train home, it would say, *I hate Slangerup*, and the simplicity of the thought is a relief.

A few weeks pass, then Christina writes to say she had a lovely time, Maggie must come again, and Maggie can't tell if she's lying or if it really is possible for people to be so different.

Maggie was fourteen the first time she was raped. But raped is my word, not hers. Many years later, she found herself sitting opposite a lady at a women's shelter. She had gone to ask about Kurt – whether the ways he'd been violent counted – but then she lost courage and asked instead if she'd been raped, all that time ago, and the woman on the other side of the table listened and said that yes, it was rape. Maggie left feeling like a fraud, because she hadn't mentioned the one thing that, to her, was the truly unbearable question: that she'd got wet, had opened herself to him.

She was fourteen, as I mentioned, and her mother had just kicked her out. One night, when she'd thought her mother would be late from work, she had brought home a boy. They'd got drunk on cherry wine and shared a few sickly-sweet kisses when all of a sudden her mum was in the doorway telling her she had to leave. The street felt very empty the next morning as she stood there with her rucksack. All she could think of was to find a man who'd let her stay with him, but she didn't know where to start. She was walking down Vesterbrogade when she saw the poster. Campsite in Jutland, everybody welcome.

\*

She chain-smoked in the train toilet until the threats on the other side of the door turned serious, then she got off at Odense and waited an hour for the next train. Learning from her original mistake, she changed toilet every time the train stopped. When at last she reached her station, she found it was nothing but a small windswept building ringed by grazing cows. The sun was high and the tarmac on the platform warm against her thighs when she sat down and arrayed the contents of her make-up bag in front of her, took out her compact and started getting ready.

The campsite was in a beautiful spot between two hills, and beyond them was the sea. Children were everywhere, the women wore long, loose dresses, and Maggie began to feel nervous. She felt exposed in her tight clothes. Grotesque. What she really wanted was to go back home, but it was too late for that. She thought of her mother, and it stung to remember that Maggie had called her a stupid old bitch before she'd slammed the door behind her.

That night, people gathered around the bonfire. Maggie, who had been wandering the campsite by herself all afternoon, looked around for a man. Scattergun at first, sprinkling a little of herself everywhere, but then eventually she decided on a young man with messy hair and a vaguely silly but also charming face. She sat down close to him and said her parents had died, that she was looking for a tent to spend the night. He shared a big tent with his family – she'd be welcome to join them, he said.

*

As it grew dark she went into the tent, expecting him to follow, but he didn't: his uncle did instead. He lay down next to her. He put his hand on her cheek, and she moved it away.

There must have been a misunderstanding. She tried to convey this with an apologetic smile, as though she were manning her body's reception desk. He muttered something, some mush of words, twisted his hand out of her grasp and put it back on her body, lifted up her top and found her breast with his mouth. Still she remained polite and full of apologies, good arguments – she felt it was her responsibility to explain, since she had put herself in his tent and given him the wrong impression – and her reasoning was that she was too young and he too old, that it wasn't a good look for either of them. Then she strained, trying to push his face away from her stomach, said no and please, but he gave her a pulpy smile, said something warm and sticky in her ear, something disgusting, and grabbed her wrist with one hand as he pulled her knickers aside with the other, pushing in two fingers. Up came a terrible wave from below. She lay still, and felt her body betray her. She got wet. His dick slid inside her easily. She has no words for what happened before he came and rolled away. Seconds later he was snoring. Hatred, shame, fear and desire interwove, were spun inside her into a lifelong conviction. She understood in that moment that violence and sex are the same thing. But she believed that the mixing of the two came from some place deep within herself, and not from anything external. Her groin throbbed and her heart pounded wildly, her head was dizzy, and then she closed herself up again with the brief, hard thought: We are alone in the world. All we have is the will to keep moving forward.

The first thing to do was to leave the camp unseen. She didn't stop until she reached the road, where she sat on the edge of the roadside ditch and lit a cigarette. It felt like she ought to cry, but she couldn't. She thought vaguely, almost abstractly, about where she was going to sleep. It was more a question that possessed the body and that drove it on than a question with an answer. She got up and stuck out her thumb. From the passenger seat, she gazed out at Jutland, dense-black and sea-sodden, stretching with a slow and unreal matter-of-factness in all directions around the car.

She was nineteen when she was raped the second time. Though she isn't sure what happened exactly. She had gone to Andy's Bar alone. A man in cowboy boots was sitting on one of the stools – he looked like a mug. An easy mark. She told one of her stories. It might have been the one where she was the exiled daughter of a Russian nobleman, a lady who commanded a vast fortune that was sadly useless in this country, where there wasn't much to spend it on. She woke up on the pavement on Sølvgade. Dawn was breaking and she was very cold. It took her a minute or two to realise it was her own blood on the paving stones. At the hospital they said someone had beaten her, and that the bruising on her arms and chest suggested she had been held down, had presumably resisted. They could tell that there had been sexual activity. She nodded, putting on an attentive expression. It felt like sitting an exam. What she really wanted was to go outside and have a smoke and start forgetting what had already been forgotten, but she knew it would seem wrong to them, suspicious, if she said she didn't want to know what had happened. Then at last they let her leave, and she went home.

Afterwards, most of the time, she managed not to think about it. That same afternoon she went to the park with a friend and laughed off her swollen face. Yeah, she was drunk last night, got knocked about a bit. But the fear arrived in sudden flashes. He could be anywhere. She might not recognise his face, but he would recognise hers. He could be sitting right there, right now, owning the moment she thinks is hers.

By the time a few years had gone by, she'd had sex with so many men that she often passed them on the street without being aware that they had recognised her. A man's face was a hole from which money could be drawn. Now when she opened the little compartments in the chest of drawers in her bedsit, there was always cash to be found. Shops opened their doors to her, she bought, bought, bought – stole too, still, although she had the money to buy. A short dress clamped under her arm and hidden beneath her jacket, while she paid for three dresses on the counter. A pair of shoes as well, silver.

She takes a taxi, filling it with the heavy scent of amber perfume. When she reaches the flat, the man she met a few days earlier decides to show off his new vacuum cleaner. He flips the switch and holds it out to her, look at the suction on that, and to make it even clearer he puts the mouth against his own arm and sucks up a little of his skin. Maggie doesn't know what to make of this performance. She's drinking red wine she assumes is expensive, and behind the arrogance of her expression it feels like the bottom dropping out of a bucket, like her hips can barely contain the water, and she laughs. Her plan is to stay for at least a week, to fill a gap that has appeared between other options.

She is at the mercy, that much she knows, of all these men with their vacuum cleaners and their drooping doggish faces, but what else is she supposed to do, take a job at a factory, clock in at five a.m.? It would never work. There's no place on the regular job market for someone like her, who can spend a whole day crying or flat out on the grass somewhere, awash with anxiety, who would never, ever be able to show up on time or really pay attention to instructions. She'd be no use to an employer, and anyway, if she does have to be of use – and that's the law – she'd rather tell herself she's choosing how. At least this way she can't get sacked. She's been through that three times, twice as a nanny and once as a sales assistant, always after just a few days on the job. She did her best when they broke the news, controlling her face and her tears until she got outside, where she let them fall. The humiliation of being sacked is what it is – she's long since given up on pride – but the *money*. Money is a space that extends far beyond the capacity for pain.

The following morning he goes to work. He's an architect, apparently – he showed her some drawings last night. She's a little uneasy, glad he's gone, because it turns out he squeaks like, well, like a little baby mouse in bed, and when he fell asleep she got up and shivered at the thought of the sound, sat in his kitchen and felt none of the euphoria she normally feels on the first night in a stranger's home.

In the park downstairs the roses are in bloom, powerfully fragrant. She sits on a bench and watches a squirrel dart up and down a tree trunk, somehow moved at the sight of this small red-glinting friend. Yes, of course, she replies to a woman who asks for a cigarette, and stares after her until she's out of sight entirely through the gate. Then, with the lightness of a hangover, her mind swims off into an image-less nostalgia.

One night she knocks on the door of a friend she hasn't seen in a very long time. The mother answers: Yes, please, come in. They sit down at the kitchen table. It's a warm night, the windows are open. Nørrebro, which had seemed like such a desert to her that night, is carried in on soporific waves of sound from the street. Her friend's mother slowly smokes a cigarette. Her expression is mild, interested, indulgent. You can almost see it quivering in the air around her, the pleasure she takes in this vision of herself, this languid cigarette, in letting this strange, wild child into her home. But Maggie knows she can't stay long. In a matter of days, the pleasure will give way to an unspoken but tangible frustration – she's a single mum, she has a child of her own to think of, there are mouths to feed, and there's the messy sofa Maggie will forget to tidy in the mornings.

The next day Maggie goes to see the council. She sits at a desk and gives a brilliant performance of a lonely child – which, in fact, she still is, but there's an art to playing it in a way that ticks the right boxes on the paperwork. Success. The caseworker puts an arm around her, and together they walk down Åboulevarden. There's a room she can have, a place for homeless young women.

She ends up living next to Tina, who never leaves her room and spends all day listening to songs from *The Jungle Book*. That Baloo one plays constantly. From time to time, Tina's parents come to visit. They sit across from their daughter in the common room while Tina flips through magazines and shows them the things she wants. Some hair clips, a purse in the shape of a starfish. Her voice is too thin to carry the rage out of her body when her parents tell her no – it cracks and turns to air. Maggie feels a certain sympathy for Tina, but the minute she lets it fill her body it transforms into disgust.

On the other side of her is Lone. Maggie rarely hangs out with girls, so her mind buzzes with wellbeing when she lets a whole day pass through her in Lone's room. They read passages from each other's books, take turns putting water on for coffee. Did you know, asks Lone, that Elsa Morante co-directed several of Pasolini's films? And Maggie says no, oh wait actually yeah, she had heard that, she'd just forgotten, and gets embarrassed and wishes she'd just stuck with no, she sounds even stupider now. She forgets about it when Lone straddles her and kisses her, first on the mouth then on the belly. Imagine if Tina saw us now, Lone giggles, and Maggie doesn't have time to laugh before Lone parts the lips of her vulva and it feels as though a warm wide road is opening.

*

But she can't do the same for Lone. She puts her face between her legs, but her mouth purses like she's thinking of sour wine gums, and after that she and Lone don't really see each other any more.

Maggie is positioned high above the station, on the balcony. She watches the trains pull in at the platforms, the people jostling out, dispersing, holding children and bags and various ideas. From where she's standing, all of that just fades away.

She set off yesterday, leaving most of her things in her room and heading for the main station, where she took the first train out of the country, destination Gothenburg. She can't be anybody's child, including the council's. She doesn't like answering to anybody about what she's doing, so she'd rather live with no one even asking.

It's give and take, she knows, the affection from the grown-ups at the council. You have to put on your tears like a costume, be grateful and renounce your former self, but you also can't become someone else entirely, because then there's nothing for them to pity or improve. But she isn't grateful for anything. She refuses to be in anybody's debt, and that's that – until she has to go crawling back to humiliate herself again for some pathetic sum of money. Still, for now that's all in the future. She has enough cash for a day or two, and something will come along after that.

Packing up was quick, as always. The essentials straight into a bag. Her shoe collection – crucial. The first thing she did after letting herself into the hotel room was to arrange all her shoes in a row. She lay on the bed as twilight fell and looked at them. The silver pair shone in the bluish room.

Later, on the balcony, she felt marvellously spaced-out, sounds swimming up to her from the square below but not demanding anything.

It wasn't until he cleared his throat that she realised there was a man standing on the balcony next to hers. He held out a pack of cigarettes across the railing. She thanked him and took one, then they were silent again.

Before he left, a little while later, going into his room and switching off the light, he gave a little speech: he'd been living at the hotel for eight years, he said, and would strongly recommend the restaurant; he'd got divorced and only meant to stay there temporarily, but time had passed, and eventually he saw no reason to move.

This morning, clutching a folder in each hand, he'd come hurrying out of the buffet just as Maggie arrived. She turned and watched his short, broad back until he was out of sight through the revolving doors. There was something of the fairy tale about him, as though he'd sprung fully formed out of the ground and set immediately about his business, darting in and out of lobbies with his varying, inscrutable documents.

In the square below, a young couple is pushing a buggy towards the station. Several times they stop to share a kiss. Maggie turns her back on them and goes into the bathroom, where she sits naked in the tub. She doesn't run the water – it's the touch of cold porcelain she wants.

She imagines writing songs about her life. She'd like to sing them the way Nico sings hers. The cigarettes have made her head dry; she's brought in a pillow to rest her neck, and now she drifts away, crossing the border unnoticed into dreams.

# SCANDINAVIAN STAR

I wake up from a dream.

In the dream I had a restaurant on a cruise ship. My speciality was shrimp, but even as I walked among the carefully laid tables, before the guests arrived, I knew I'd told a lie. What followed next was vague. Swing doors opening and closing, a series of earnest telephone calls in shifting rooms, until I landed in a helicopter on a windswept field. There was a man with an utterly generic face who briefed me on the scale of the disaster. I turned to the crew to delegate tasks, but I didn't know what I was saying. Then, zoom out. I saw myself standing on the helicopter's bottom step. I was waving my arms – I looked upset. Nothing could be heard above the noise of wind and machine. That was the last thing in my dream, the distinct sensation of wind.

I only became aware of the fatal fire on the *Scandinavian Star* passenger ferry long after the fact. I was two years old when it happened, and probably twenty or so when I first read an article about a man whose family had died in the blaze.

He'd been investigating the circumstances around it for years, believing the police hadn't done enough. They'd never considered there might have been a financial motive behind it.

Instead, the Norwegian police had named a lorry driver as the prime suspect, a man who had died in the fire himself. It stood to reason, or so it seemed, that a mentally unstable man with previous convictions for arson might take it into his head to do it again. But they had no evidence, and the case was dropped.

A picture to accompany the article: the amateur detective seated among the stacks of documents he had gathered on the case over the years. In my memory, the stacks take up a whole room. It was as though, in those growing mounds of paper, he had made the dead material again, as though he'd brought them back to fill the void they'd left behind.

Some years later, a retired marine inspector came forward to say that the official report was in direct contradiction to what he'd seen during his investigations immediately after the event.

On 7 April 1990, at least four fires broke out on the *Scandinavian Star*.

The first was discovered by some passengers and put out. Then, not long after that, another: a fire that spread fast and claimed the lives of 159 people, the one referred to as the primary fire. Once all the surviving passengers had been evacuated, and long after the work of extinguishing the blaze was underway, at least two more broke out.

The official explanation offered by the Norwegian police was that these latter fires were flare-ups linked to the primary fire. Which was precisely what the marine inspector was now disputing, as in fact the fire commander on the scene at the time had done as well. During his investigation, he had found clear evidence that the fires which occurred after the primary incident had been started deliberately.

This was a big claim, for two reasons. For one, the lorry driver had died during the primary fire, so he couldn't possibly have started the subsequent two. For another, all the surviving passengers had been evacuated by the time they broke out. The only people still on the ship, apart from the firefighters, were a small group of crew members who were supposed to be helping put out the blaze. Any fires that broke out after that point must therefore have been started by someone on the crew.

There was something very well-scrubbed and self-assured about the marine inspector. The reason he hadn't spoken up before, he said, was because he'd held a senior position within the Danish Maritime Authority, and hence 'his hands were tied'.

During his original testimony in court, he said, he had been asked specifically about the first two fires, but had neglected to mention his observations about the third and fourth. He had communicated his findings to the police immediately after the investigation as well as subsequently in a private meeting, but in court he had simply answered the questions he was asked.

It wasn't until twenty-six years later, two years after the Norwegian police had finally withdrawn the charges against the lorry driver, and only after his own retirement, that he broke the silent settlement he'd made with himself.

The inspector baffled me. He seemed to consider himself an upstanding, conscientious type of person, and it occurred to me that the same self-perception compelling him to speak out now was also what had enabled him to stay silent for all those years.

There is a silence, a dread of coming across as stupid, that sets in where money is concerned.

I'm not quite sure of the right words to use. What is the difference between a company, a business and a firm? Are there differences, or do they all mean the same thing?

When I read about the companies involved in what happened on the *Scandinavian Star*, I cannot picture rooms. I don't know if there were offices, employees marching down corridors, jumbled wires, a big warm fax machine whining as information poured in. I don't know if any of that was needed for the operation to work. I don't know if there was an actual address somewhere behind all the decoy ones.

I know the company that officially claimed ownership of the *Scandinavian Star* wasn't registered anywhere, nor had it notified the authorities of the address it later gave in court, after the fire. In fact, the company didn't actually own the ship at all.

\*

Like I said, no rooms.

Still, I have to use these words, although I'll never really understand what they mean.

It was the mid-eighties, and Ole B. Hansen and Henrik Johansen had just set up a shipping corporation. They ran the Vognmandsruten, a ferry route across the strait between the Danish islands of Zealand and Funen. Hansen was the CEO while Johansen, who had made his money in property speculation, was the main investor and shareholder. He owned the Vognmandsruten through another company, the VR Group. As ever, when it came to Johansen's businesses, the structure was somewhat arcane. The VR Group was subdivided into a number of smaller businesses, but all of them were owned by members of Johansen's family.

The Vognmandsruten managed to hugely undercut their competitor, DSB, on ticket price. They accomplished this in all the usual ways: lower wages, poorer working conditions, a fast and loose attitude towards safety regulations. Several unions banned their members from taking jobs on the route. Over the years, numerous stories appeared in the media about the Vognmandsruten's creative approach to safety and the treatment of its employees.

\*

Perhaps Hansen and Johansen had ties with investors in Florida even then. Employees would, from time to time, receive cheques issued in Miami.

On 1 March 1990, Johansen sold the Vognmandsruten to a Danish investment fund. The price was 369 million kroner.

In the months preceding the sale of the Vognmandsruten, Johansen's VR Group opened negotiations with an American company. Its name was SeaEscape, and it was headquartered in Florida but registered in the Bahamas. These negotiations concerned the purchase of a passenger ferry called the *Scandinavian Star*. SeaEscape had originally been founded by Niels-Erik Lund, a Dane who had previously been CEO. By 1990, however, he was no longer running the company, acting instead as an independent broker helping SeaEscape to sell ships to Denmark. It was Lund who facilitated the sale of the *Scandinavian Star* to the VR Group.

In January 1990, the initial sales agreement was drawn up. The VR Group would pay a deposit of 2.5 million dollars for the vessel by 16 February, and the remaining 19.2 million in late March, on which date the ownership would be officially transferred. When the first deadline passed and Johansen still hadn't paid the deposit, it was extended by a week. But again, Johansen failed to pay. In late March, by which time the whole sum was due to have been paid, SeaEscape still had not received any money for the ship.

*

Nonetheless, the company agreed to transfer the ship to Johansen and the VR Group. In an agreement signed on 30 March, SeaEscape stipulated that they would remain the registered owner of the ship, since the payment hadn't yet gone through, and that in the event of damage to the vessel, any insurance money would be paid to them. The agreement also set out a new deadline for payment: the money would be transferred by 6 April at the latest, or the *Scandinavian Star* would be returned to SeaEscape. On 1 April, passengers travelling the Frederikshavn–Oslo route boarded the *Scandinavian Star* for the first time, and it set sail. Six days later, on 6 April, Johansen again broke the terms of the contract: he still hadn't paid. He was granted another three days' reprieve.

While Johansen had handled the negotiations, it was Hansen, as CEO, who had travelled to Florida to inspect the ship. It was also Hansen who agreed with SeaEscape that some of the current crew could continue working on the ship. The acting chief engineer, Heinz Steinhauser, was tasked with drawing up a list of crew members he thought should remain.

In mid-March – before the *Scandinavian Star* was formally handed over to the VR Group – it had set sail for Cuxhaven in Germany, where it was due to be refurbished for use on the Frederikshavn to Oslo route. According to several employees who boarded the ship at Cuxhaven, it was nowhere near ready for the type of crossing the VR Group had in mind for it. Many cabins had been left unused for a long time and were in need of renovation. It would be impossible to have the ship in a fit state by the deadline Hansen and Johansen had set.

On 30 March, the same day SeaEscape signed an agreement to transfer the *Scandinavian Star* to the VR Group, SeaEscape bought the ship from the Swedish company Stena Line. How they had been able to enter into a contract to sell a vessel they didn't yet formally own is unclear. From 1984 until 30 March 1990, SeaEscape had been leasing the ship from Stena Line, with a contract in place that gave them the option to eventually buy it at a price offset against the instalments they had already paid. SeaEscape bought the ship from Stena Line for 10.3 million dollars. After deducting the money already paid, the actual sum was only half that. They signed a contract to transfer the ship to the VR Group the very same day, but at a price more than double what Stena Line had sold it for. The VR Group had agreed to buy it for 21.7 million dollars.

In the aftermath of the fire, this caused bewilderment among commentators and the victims' relatives. Could Stena Line really have misjudged the ship's market value so dramatically that they asked for less than half of what SeaEscape was able to sell it on for the very same day? Or was Johansen well aware that he had agreed to buy the ship for a sum monumentally above its true value? Was the VR Group's failure to pay and SeaEscape's forbearance due to the fact that both parties knew the deal would never actually go ahead?

At any rate, the new sales price meant the ship could now be insured for a lot more money. A comprehensive policy was taken out, covering up to 24 million dollars and expiring on 7 April 1990.

When the ship caught fire in the early hours of 7 April 1990, it was not, as Johansen testified in court, his company – K/S Scandinavian Star – who owned it. SeaEscape was still registered as the vessel's legal owner in the Bahamas, with the 'managing owner' recorded as Niels-Erik Lund. The insurance money would go to SeaEscape, and – in case of catastrophic damage – amounted to 24 million dollars, although we'll never know precisely how much was paid out, because according to the insurance company the documents were shredded shortly after.

On 1 April 1990, a few days before the fire, Lund – ex-CEO of SeaEscape and the man who had brokered the sale of the *Scandinavian Star* – founded a new company: ISP. It was ISP who bought the wreck, and ISP who went on to operate the vessel after it was rebuilt.

In the years following the arson, the VR Group and ISP were involved in various other projects together. ISP's chief technical officer was Heinz Steinhauser, former chief engineer on the *Scandinavian Star*. Among other things, it was Steinhauser's behaviour during the blaze that made the incident commander believe key crew members were trying to obstruct his team's efforts.

In 1991, SeaEscape filed for bankruptcy in the USA. During the court proceedings, company shareholders described two other deals signed with Henrik Johansen immediately after the fire, outlining a scheme by which Johansen would 'buy' the ships – owning them on paper in order to claim tax benefits in Denmark – while SeaEscape would remain the de facto operator.

These statements were only brought to wider public attention in 1997, when Norwegian and Danish journalists published a series of investigations into who actually owned the *Scandinavian Star*. This was the first time the public learned that Johansen had lied in court, and that his company had never even owned the vessel.

It makes me dizzy, reading about commerce. Dizzy, reading about companies with overlapping clusters of owners, all buying and selling from each other. Money that both does and does not change hands.

When I was at primary school and my maths teacher took away the blocks from his desk and started writing symbols on the board instead of simply moving the blocks around, even then it felt like I was overheating. What is four, if not four of something? If you add two, but you had nothing concrete to begin with, only a number, don't you still have nothing? I tried explaining to my maths teacher what it was I didn't understand. He beckoned me up to the desk, took out the blocks again. What happens, he asked, if I move two blocks over to this side of my desk, where there are already four? You have six blocks, I counted. Then he repeated the sum on the board, turning back to me as though he'd explained something. *See, it's the same.* But to me it wasn't the same. I flushed hot, my chest ached. *Do you understand it now?* I lied, I said I understood. But still I couldn't hold back my tears. I stood at the front of the class and cried.

\*

When I read about commerce, about millions of dollars that split and grow, vanish and grow, it makes me dizzy.

I try anyway. I want to understand.

I know this is the tactic of the businessman. He triumphs, operating in a language that silences. When I think I'm being stupid, he triumphs.

Over the course of the eighties, SeaEscape had a remarkable number of fires break out on their cruise ships. The *Scandinavian Star*, the *Scandinavian Sea*, the *Scandinavian Sun* – all of them caught alight. These fires started and spread in ways much like the *Star*'s, although there were no deaths.

On 7 April 1990, 159 people died as a result of the fire. Twenty-eight children. The youngest was just a few months old.

I think about my own child. I'll be picking her up from nursery soon, and I begin to cry. These are strange tears. These are rage and grief and love in one.

If the *Star* was set on fire so that SeaEscape could pocket the insurance money, they probably didn't mean for anyone to die. It was a *mistake*. The passengers were supposed to be evacuated, and then they'd leave the ship to burn.

But evacuation plans cost money. Fire drills take time to hold. Man hours. Wages. So they didn't bother.

\*

Henrik Johansen, Ole B. Hansen and Hugo Larsen, the captain of the *Scandinavian Star*, were each sentenced in the Maritime and Commercial Court to six months' imprisonment for infringing maritime safety legislation.

Hansen never served his time. He went into exile in Spain, impunity incarnate. The impunity only ever granted to his class.

One hundred and fifty-nine people died. It is all too possible they died so that others could profit.

There is no comfort to be had in telling ourselves these cases are rare.

If there's anything rare about this case, it is only that the victims of capitalism (assuming we ignore the ones not even counted as victims: plants, insects, fungi, fish) aren't usually located in Scandinavia.

In Oslo they've built a memorial for the victims of the arson, but nowhere in Scandinavia is there a memorial for the textile workers who were victims of the factory collapses in Bangladesh and Cambodia, even though Scandinavian companies were among those that kept the factories running until the roofs fell in.

And yet, although nothing in this version of the world is equally distributed, although the West has by and large outsourced its pain, some of that suffering still remains within our borders. Even in the West, people are paying with their lives to keep the system going. If you're lower class, you don't live as long. Even here.

No. Death is *not* a mistake. It's part of the deal.

When a whole village gets cancer after working with pesticides on an American-owned banana plantation, death and disease may not have been the point, exactly, but those people's lives were a sacrifice the banana company was always willing to make.

Death is not a mistake. A murder is a murder, even if the murderer is out for money not for blood.

If it's true, and I believe it is, that the fire on the *Scandinavian Star* was started for the purpose of financial gain, then those 159 people didn't die because a few individuals were cynical enough to take a terrible risk. They died for an idea.

In order for one group to profit, somebody and something else may have to die. That is the idea.

If one wants to add, one must subtract elsewhere.

Capitalism is a massacre.

But we are alive, and we can end capitalism.

And what of Kurt and Maggie? Kurt's investments had bound their lives to the fire long before it even happened.

He had put his earnings into the Vognmandsruten, but before the *Star* was even set alight he lost it all to men who knew much better than he did how to turn a sum of money into more of it.

As for Maggie, if there was fire inside her it stirred only as a premonition. She died in Odense Hospital just six months before the blaze broke out.

# A GREAT WHITE-GLITTERING HULK

It's raining when Maggie gets off the bus. She barely gets through a third of her cigarette before it's sodden and goes out. She could sit down somewhere, let the deluge and the hours pass, put off the appointment until another day. But then she does what she must: she walks, hunched and furious against the rain, towards the hospital.

It was some months ago, the first time she woke up in unfamiliar pain. It felt like her eye was being jerked back into her head on a wire of burning ice. She jumped out of bed, kicking her legs as though invaded by some force that could be driven out with corresponding violence. The pain went on for what felt like many minutes, then she was back inside her old, quiet head, and it was hard to believe she had ever been gone. Bewildered, a faint haze now between herself and her habits, she tiptoed into the kitchen and placed the coffee filter and the grounds gingerly into the machine, trying not to make a sound. Whatever it was, this alien rage that had arisen inside her, she had to be careful so as not to wake it up again. Each time the pain resurfaced after that it came as a shock, but eventually she grew accustomed to it. She learned to lie down and not move so much as a finger, to think rhythmically of the sea, to swim out stroke by stroke into the pain until abruptly it had ended.

A few months after that, her left arm began to tingle. On and off, at first, then all the time. It wasn't impossible to use it, but she had to concentrate on what she wanted the arm to do – focus, for example, on the scrubbing brush, not let it out of her mind until her hand had reached out and grasped it. One day, out of nowhere, she couldn't feel her big toe. She pressed and pressed it with her finger and eventually took a knife and made a scratch, but nothing. For the first time she faced up to the question she'd been trying to ignore, and with it came a wave of fear. For a day or two she circled the telephone, raging at it, thinking it might be the thing that wanted her dead, until at last she called the doctor. When she got through to the receptionist, she said she had athlete's foot. Chronic, a nasty case. Some days later, in the waiting room, almost burning up in her chair, she'd been on the verge of leaving several times, feet planted on the floor, ready to rise and go; but she stayed. After the doctor examined her foot – it only needed some ointment, which Maggie would never have bothered to smear on anyway – she enquired about Maggie's health more generally. Fine, said Maggie, everything's fine. Then she mentioned how she couldn't feel her big toe, and then all the other things.

She has considered telling Kurt. It's been on the tip of her tongue every time they sit across from one another at the dinner table in silence. This morning, as she went off down the gravel track towards the bus stop and the hospital, she stopped several times. She imagined going back and falling into his arms, imagined there might be some embrace that would transport them back, she's not sure to when; or perhaps they could begin anew. And then every time she shook the thought away, set off again, only to stop once more a moment later. On the bus she couldn't hold back her tears. Mile by mile she grew more distant from the man she had distanced herself from long ago, but now, when death had arrived to ask her what she'd made of her life, she realised it was Kurt she'd wanted all along.

She's already had enough of the young doctor's haircut. It's sloppy and arrogant, and she's decided these things about him before he's even shaken her hand and said his name in the strangely jovial way of youth, offered to explain a little about what she can expect today. They walk further down the corridor, then he opens the door to the room where her fate will be decided. It's a great white-glistening hulk of a thing, the machine which will photograph her brain, and in the middle of it is a hole where she'll be slid inside and must lie very still until the scan is finished. An hour, or thereabouts. The machine creaks and howls as it gets to work. It's a violation, two young men there peering through a screen into her open head, and her lying motionless inside the hole in the machine, afraid. When it's over and they've found a bed for her, she calls Sofie. She's not sure where to start. She rambles. There were these headaches for a while, and then this scan; then Sofie cuts her off and demands to know if this is serious. Yes, I think it is, she says.

A few days later she is back in the doctor's office. He looks up from his paperwork, tucks a lock of hair behind his ear, inhales the air loudly through his nose and blows it back out loudly through his mouth. Right, he begins. It's his job to explain the results of the scan and give her a realistic picture of where they go from here. Maggie, who has already realised that where they go from here is nowhere good, says nothing. She barely listens as the doctor explains what tumours are, and why the location of this one makes it hard to operate, that her chances aren't great. He's about to take some pictures out of the folder on the desk when Maggie stands up, stops him with a thank you and walks out. She'd rather not know any more. It's the only privilege she has, that she doesn't have to know what he knows, and he's not taking that away from her. She would prefer, at the very least, that her head remains closed to itself.

Chances, she says to Sofie later that day, because she wants to say something to make her daughter laugh, it's so funny the way they say chances and not chance. I mean, would you rather have several not-great chances or just one?

She won't be going home again, not now, but she can't cope with ringing Kurt. It would be easier to tell a total stranger that she's going to die than him. Perhaps she senses, too, that her death will be near impossible for him to survive, perhaps she can't bear the thought. Instead, it's Sofie's job to keep her father in the loop. Every day, without her mother's permission, she calls him and asks if he'll be visiting the hospital soon, and he says yes, maybe later today, definitely tomorrow. But he doesn't visit. He just can't drag himself into that hospital, he can't.

He really *can't*. Sometimes, when you can't bear something, there is no choice but to leave it be. During the months Maggie is in hospital, he wakes up every day with a start, immediately in motion. He can't stay in; he must go out. He forgets to eat several days in a row. Suddenly, at a petrol station, he remembers food and his stomach screams, hollow. He points at almost everything they've got on display, carries it all out to a bench, where he takes a few bites of hotdog before the dry bread swells in his mouth. It feels as though he's being choked. He regurgitates the bread into a bin, throws the rest of what he's bought in there as well.

At home he avoids pauses. He keeps his body moving, walking into the barn, doing a lap around the yard, into the old stable block and along the stalls, which are crammed with all sorts of rubbish, this and that, things he once thought might come in handy. It seems silly now. He rushes out, down to the wild meadow where he used to take Turner, and realises he can't be there either.

Then he can't hold out any more. He gets into the car and races the short stretch into Nyborg. He hates himself as he climbs the miserable stairwell, and hates himself when Lene opens the door, with a look on her face as though the mere sight of him is an insult. He starts to cry. He's much too big, standing on that tiny landing – Lene has no option but to break all her promises and hold him. A reserved embrace at first, then she softens against her will, hugs him close. As he lies under a blanket on her sofa, he feels life come trickling back. It starts at the feet, a spreading warmth that travels through the body. He is drowsy.

By the time he wakes up, half a day has passed. At first he can't make sense of what he's hearing, but as he grows more alert he can distinguish Bent's voice from Lene's. Bent pulls a chair up to the sofa, and it's nice, they're both equally shy. Bent looks down at the floor and asks him only simple questions. Would Kurt like a cigarette? Would he like a cold compress on his forehead? Kurt says no to that, although he's sweating buckets.

Taking turns, Bent and Lene seize on this or that, something they could all do with right now. They nip down to the corner shop to buy cake and crisps, which they toss onto the coffee table in an off-hand gesture that isn't meant to signal off-handedness, but rather that there's more where that came from, that they know life's shit, but at least they'll grab you anything you need from the shop.

Hours pass. They leave the TV on, talking over it or, suddenly engrossed in something, watching for a while. No one tells Kurt what to do or say. He's grateful, but as night comes on his conscience gets to him. He's not the one dying. He's not the one lying in hospital with tubes in his arms, or whatever it was that Sofie said the other day. He drives back to the farm and is instantly restless again. All night he's in those stalls. High time to sort them out.

The worst part is, he can't remember Maggie's face. He must have got too used to it, and now it's beyond recall. He tries. The nose, that's sort of how it was, he thinks, the lips – no, he can't make them fit, it all vanishes. One day over morning coffee, he tells Fatih about the night he and Maggie first met, but realises mid-telling that the narrative is empty now, well-worn words turned stark, because they've lost their connection to her. He stalks out of the barn in a rage, leaving his employees to the buses, which are taken out less and less often now, because he only picks up the phone in bursts.

There is one memory Kurt *can* feel, and he guards it jealously, perpetually afraid that overuse will suck it dry. It was one night not long after they met, they were at a party. Maggie insisted they separate – she wanted to be alone on the dancefloor, but to have him near by. He watched her walk away and leave him behind. He felt attached to her still, as if by a string or – how to put it? – it was as though he had acquired a new and solitary sense, one devoted to her alone.

Maggie can't get out of bed unaided these days. She must be turned frequently to prevent bedsores, which makes her feel as though she's in some sort of recipe. Yesterday, while she was being helped to the bathroom, the nurse dropped her on the floor. She guided her immediately back onto the toilet seat, apologising, and Maggie said, Oh, these things happen. It was only later that day, when Sofie demanded to know why she was covered in bruises, when she saw Sofie struggling not to cry, only then that it hit her how much she'd felt like a useless lump of meat when the nurse – who could hardly be blamed for making one mistake, one out of a thousand times – had apologised and then left her alone, shutting the door behind her.

Sometimes, Maggie thinks she'd rather death just came and got it over with. It can have her. But there are other times, like now, when Sofie's with her, that Maggie begs – begs someone, anyone – for all the time she can get. She picks her arm up slowly off the mattress, reaching out to Sofie, and Sofie holds the glass of juice up like a question – is it this you want? But Maggie doesn't want juice now. She wants to tell Sofie that she'll miss her. Sofie takes her hand

and squeezes it, looks away and up at the TV, its pictures broadcast somewhere by the ceiling. I'll miss you too, she says.

Although she cannot give that grief a name, Maggie misses Kurt as well. But he still can't give her what she once dreamed in him. Then language moves beyond her grasp, drifting into morphine, into pain, and she enters a world of thought I'll never know. She's there for days. And then she dies.

# A FEW HARSH WORDS

It's late summer now. Clouds of flies and bees; they swarm around the plums squashed on the lawn. A swallow's nest was damaged in a storm a week or two ago. Kurt was bitter about it for days, thin-lipped. He'd been dreaming about those baby birds and couldn't wrap his head around how such a thing could happen.

Maggie pours herself another cup of coffee. It's bothering her that Sofie won't just come out and say what she wants to eat on her birthday. I don't know, surprise me, was her answer, and Maggie is nervous. A year or two ago, Maggie called home excitedly from a phone box to ask if Sofie had seen that gorgeous dress in the window of La Vita. Sofie had seen it, and she also thought it was gorgeous, so Maggie went into the shop and bought it. It's for my daughter, she told the amiably uninterested sales assistant, my daughter loves yellow. She felt very specifically like a floating cucumber as she made her way through town and to the bus stop with the bag. But at home it turned out that wasn't the one Sofie had been thinking of at all, it was another yellow dress. My body's going to look all wrong in that, she said, eyes welling with tears, I'll look like a sack.

Maggie tried to breathe evenly and keep from crying herself.

It's not a pleasant memory. Maggie dismisses it by chiding herself over something else – she's forgotten to water the plants *again* today – and goes outside. Her one and only flowerbed is parched. By the time it occurred to her she should be watering them more often during the heatwave, it was already too late. She can't recall the names of the things she once planted there. Still, something comes up every spring, and it's enough to keep her happy.

She snips off a few desiccated blossoms. It is necessary to crouch. She doesn't want to risk bending over, not with Kurt around. For many years after they first started living together, he'd come bounding over whenever she bent down and bump his crotch against her backside, making funny noises. She never liked it, but said nothing, except what is always communicated when a woman falls silent and rigid. At first she was afraid of hurting his feelings, later just afraid of him, until in time the fear had become routine.

Kurt and Maggie met at the pub. Maggie had decided she wanted to be a singer. The guitar lessons were exhausting. There was something rigid about learning an instrument, something fundamentally dizzying about having to place your fingers in *exactly* the right formation, never being allowed any leeway. It was the same reason she'd been sacked from the shop. There is no leeway when it comes to money, and if there is no leeway, she doesn't stand a chance. How is she supposed to know what fifty minus thirty-three and a half is, it's too confusing.

Still, she stuck with the lessons, overcoming her embarrassment, for as long as it took. She kept not understanding how it was supposed to go, and the teacher must have thought she was an idiot, but she'd promised herself she wouldn't give up. Now she thought she'd learned enough, and singing, well, that she could do already. Unlike the guitar, that laborious instrument, it was as easy as running into the sea. She convinced the owner of the local pub to let her play a few nights in a row, and it was at one of those performances that Kurt came up to her, put a warm hand on her shoulder and said, Thank you, that was great. She knew immediately. There's no explaining it. In his face, which was very handsome, she saw her own child.

He was headed elsewhere with some friends, and although he didn't explicitly invite her to join them he let her know with a lingering look that he wanted her to. She walked at the back of the group, chatting to a boring man who warned her that he could tell which way the wind was blowing, but Maggie should know his friend was happily married, couldn't live without his wife, in fact, even if sometimes late at night he convinced himself he could. Maggie said a few disdainful words about marriage, not very many, because she was too drunk, and in any case her whole attention was focused on trying to catch what *he* was talking about ahead of them.

She'd been in love once before. But that was when she was sixteen. She hadn't thought she was capable of it any more. Or she'd forgotten love even existed.

They found a pub in Christianshavn, not far from where Kurt lived. She kept shuffling closer to him on the bench – this was her job now, since he obviously wanted to pretend he hadn't made the first move. In return he bought the beer, more and more of it, until the room was spinning for both of them, and then Kurt pulled her up to prove he really had been in Argentina as a ship's boy, that he really could dance the tango. A table got knocked over as they danced, and they were both chucked out.

\*

All was quiet by the canal, the air soft. Things were different outside – they couldn't just pick up where they'd left off at the pub. Out here they felt the seriousness of what they were doing. Reality broke like morning. They sat for a while on a bench and stared out. What do you think about the squatters? asked Kurt, and Maggie, who had no idea what Kurt was talking about, said she didn't know. Then she couldn't wait any longer and climbed onto his lap.

She woke up sore next morning. Sex on a bench. There were grazes on her knees, and she decided he would contact her before the grazes had healed. He *had* to.

A few days passed, then the first letter arrived. A postcard in an envelope:

You're wonderful. Can I see you again? Kurt

The day after, before Maggie had answered the first, a second letter came:

I should tell you I have a wife and child. But you know that. Kurt

To Maggie, the wife and child were an abstraction. A minor inconvenience to be overcome. Sometimes, to Kurt's annoyance, she'd take up her position on the bench across from their home as early as the afternoon. If she stood on the bench she could see into their living room; but she'd promised she at least would not do that. At long last, after dinner, the light went on in the landing: he was on his way down. They walked on opposite sides of the road, each breathless, until they were far enough away from the house to fall into each other's arms.

One day, on the quay, he said maybe he'd been on the wrong track from the start. With his wife. Ulla was so different from Maggie, so adamant and cold-blooded, surely not the right woman for him at all. But then his face fell shut, withdrawing into a pain that Maggie, who had no experience of marriage or even a long-term relationship, didn't recognise. I just can't bring myself to leave her, he moaned, I can't, and Maggie's hatred of the woman flared. But she would pretend to be understanding, listened patiently to everything Kurt said, although she neither understood it nor respected it, knowing that this way he would eventually open his handsome face to her again, which he always did.

You're wild, you're so wild, he repeated. If there was a place, some small part of Maggie that knew he was making a myth out of her, a myth it would be impossible to live up to, she would not acknowledge it.

What is love? Maggie is looking at me with a face like an empty prayer. As though only the form of the prayer were left, an infernal outline.

I don't know, sweet Maggie. You tell me, and I'll write it down.

I had just made him mine. I had dreams of taking a trip far away with him, but he thought we should stay in Denmark, so I chose Møn. We took a walk along the cliff, enormously white from certain angles in the sun. I walked ahead of him down narrow paths. Later, we drove into town. He bought a dress for me, a purple one, I have it still. We found a pub, ate pork chops. I remember the loving way he looked at me as I spooned gravy over the potatoes. It distracted me and I went overboard with the gravy, making us both laugh. I couldn't think of anything more beautiful than him behind the wheel, a cigarette in the corner of his mouth. It looked very American. I felt so lucky. Young. You can follow each emotion as it flits across his face, that's the type of person he is. One moment it is closed, his face, and then the littlest thing – a brood of ducklings or a kind word from the woman at the till – turns it almost inside out. I loved him for that. One night he sat down suddenly on a tree stump. He looked anguished, and I thought he might have changed his mind. But then he returned from wherever he'd disappeared to, and said he would give me everything.

\*

There's one night after that I remember in particular. We were at a party. It spread across two storeys with a wide connecting staircase. I walked away from Kurt, leaving him alone for a few moments. I could hardly tear myself away, but I *wanted* to know how it felt to be apart. A quiver running through me as I stood on the dancefloor alone. We were separated by the crowd, but bound to one another by some crazed and terrible force.

Perhaps without me noticing, only six months later things had changed. We had gone to Samsø, because he had an aunt who lived there. One day, on impulse, I stepped over an electric fence and walked across one of the fields. It was quite big, and I'd been walking for a while when suddenly the buck in the field just went for me. I ran as fast as I could. I was afraid, yes, but also happy – it felt like I was running in laughter. I didn't look back until I was on the other side of the fence again. As I stood there panting, Kurt arrived in front of me. It's hard to explain. It was as though the mere sight of him cut me off from the moment I'd just experienced. That space was empty now. Suddenly nothing to tell. He asked what had happened, and I just shrugged.

We'd been together no more than a few weeks. He always woke up early, wanting sex. One morning, I didn't – I wanted just a bit more sleep. At first I didn't get it. That he was genuinely angry. I thought he was playing around, and searched for it in his expression. Somewhere behind his indignant face there had to be a trace of love, but I couldn't find it. He flung a couple of pillows at my head, making me sit up in bed. Naked confusion. When I got back home that afternoon, he'd bought flowers and champagne. He begged me not to stop loving him. That hadn't occurred to me. I wouldn't have been able to. I was bewildered. I thought he was overplaying it a bit, the part of the lovesick boy. But also that his vehemence was touching, grand.

It slipped away from me somehow. Another night, the same confusion: he was upset because I'd left a party earlier than he'd wanted to, and so he pushed me out of bed. I wanted it to be a kind of game. I climbed back up, and he pushed me out again. That second time, on the floor, I felt like a tortoise on its back. It was clumsy and embarrassing, climbing up again. The next day I was the one consoling and apologising. I tried to translate it: he was scared of losing me, that's why he was so angry, he just loved me too much. And I *must* have done something wrong, if the man I made happy was unhappy.

The first time he spat on me, we'd been sharing memories from our schooldays. He told me some of his bad memories, and I told him one of mine. I'd had sex with a slightly older man, and the next day he had waited outside the school gates to ask me out. That was what had started the campaign against me. People decided I was a slut and should be punished for it. The worst part was when someone had stopped my mother on the street, breathed heavily into her face and asked if she knew what her daughter was up to. Kurt was silent after I finished my story. I could sense him tightening around a feeling, one that wasn't good. Somehow we were in disagreement. He stood up, spat in my face and called me an ugly whore. There was a very stark silence after he had gone. Then he came back and asked me to lie down with him for a while. I was taut with self-loathing and revulsion as we lay in bed; I felt like I was going to be sick. But I could sense how desperate my refusal made him, so I gave in. We had sex. It hurt, because I was tensing against it. I had never really felt like a whore, the way people use the word, but I did then. If I have any advice for girls, it's that you should never sleep with a man who calls you that, not if you love him. It will destroy you.

I did love Kurt. I loved him boundlessly. I thought he was the only one who truly understood me. Sometimes he showed me a tenderness I don't think any human being had shown me before. It was a devotion absolute, as though I lived within him, moving his cells with my speech. I recovered my own life through his movements, but transformed. After he had carried my life, I could carry it too. And I cherished my almost limitless affection for him. I would do anything for him. I would bear anything and still offer comfort to him.

The second time he spat on me, he'd just come back from a job interview that hadn't gone well. I went to hug him and he spat on me. The third time it was because I'd said too sharply that we had to take the next exit. He pulled over, spat at me, and spat at me again when I began to cry. It slipped away from me somehow. He held me tightly up against the wall or under him in bed, destroyed my things, threatened to burn down the flat. One morning he held out a kitchen knife – I'm still not sure if he was threatening to kill himself or me. He would sometimes fly into a rage, not only if I wasn't in the mood for sex, but if I wasn't in the mood for the same kind of sex as him. He called me old and ugly, threatened to break things off with me because I didn't want anal, said he was looking forward to having sex with someone less boring. I could choose between one humiliation or the other: his fury if I said no, or letting him do what he wanted to me. I forgot there was a third option. I loved him. I didn't want to end things. There were times we were so happy, like we were caught in a storm of laughter and courage. I couldn't end things.

But somewhere in me there was doubt, working away in its own locked room. It could not be reconciled with my love and could not touch it. When, every now and then, it pushed its way up to the surface, he knew it before I did. *You don't love me any more. If you don't love me any more, it will destroy me. I will die.* Then I reassured. I comforted. I was still afraid, but it was more of a dull, wadded sense that I'd forgotten something. And I wasn't just afraid – in those moments I felt motherly and strong. I was flattered, too; he made me feel that I alone held his life in my hands, I alone could pardon or condemn. I chose to pardon. It gave me a sense of superiority that eased what those degradations had cost me.

Slowly, something else began as well. Something sheer and irreversible that transformed Kurt before my eyes. One night, when we were at a party, he was sulking. I came off the dancefloor to find him sitting alone at the table. We went outside, and I could see he wasn't happy. I told him we could do whatever he liked, go home or stay, even take a night-time walk, just the two of us. He held my eye and said that if we could do whatever he liked, he'd like to fuck me in the arse. I don't know why that was the moment, that precise moment, but for the first time I felt something new. I drew back from him. I wanted to go straight home. But it was the morning after when I really felt it, when I saw his anguished face: I knew I didn't care, not any more. Let him suffer.

I must have thought that pregnancy would put a stop to his behaviour. That it would protect me. So it shocked me all over again when it happened in the first few weeks. He called me a whore and spat on me, twisted the plate I was holding out of my hands and poured its contents over me. It must have been rice, because I remember picking the grains out of my top, one by one, mute with white-hot hatred. It was different being humiliated now that I was pregnant. It felt limitless. I thought of the growing child, and the nightmare stretched in all directions without end. I left, and he came running after me, holding out his hand to mine. I knew the look on his face so well: a plea and a menace in one. We walked in silence to the cinema. His suggestion. I got terrible cramps during the film – I thought it was a miscarriage, and I wished for it, I thought it would be fitting vengeance. I stood in the toilet at the cinema and felt victorious, wicked, riding the waves of pain in my abdomen, when suddenly I was frightened. I do want you, I do want you, I promised, and put a hand on my belly as though to hold the child inside.

*

I went to Berlin, boarding the train with no plan but to survive this fear. I found a room I could rent cheaply for a month or two. Kurt threatened to kill himself when I called him, and I hung up. I didn't know how I was going to make it the ten yards from the phone box back up the stairwell. I sat down and couldn't even cry. I must have fallen asleep. A woman who had come to use the phone reached down a hand to me and helped me up. *Du bist schwanger, das ist gut, ja?* I couldn't bring myself to meet her eye. In my room upstairs I lay in bed for days, doing nothing but watching the treetops shift in the wind outside my window. It was a high-ceilinged, dusty room that smelled sharply of urine from the shared toilet next door. One day I went to the zoo, and a marten hissed at me from inside its tiny cage. I was convinced it had to be the child, sending me a message. It's not easy to admit this, now I know it was Sofie, or what would become Sofie, but I did everything I could think of to induce a miscarriage. I drank heavily and chain-smoked. I ran up and down the stairs, not stopping even when the pain was screeching in my belly. I'd got hold of numbers, different doctors, and more than once I went down to the phone box with the bit of paper in my hand. I'd let the phone ring once or twice before I set down the receiver with a smack. I'd changed my mind, I was desperate to have the baby. I writhed in bed, begging for forgiveness. Sorry, little darling, sorry, sorry.

But yes, I did return home from Berlin. For the first time in ages, I was afraid of being alone. I needed Kurt. It terrified me that I was no longer merely in love with him but needed him to survive. What had protected me so far was the belief that I didn't really need a man at all – that my chances were better alone. That I could board a train at any time and soon be thinking of the whole thing as a strange and distant flower, one inexplicability among many. Now I threw myself into our arguments with an abandon I had never known before. Gone was the pious, masochistic complacency of my silence, my forgiveness. There were no limits and no endpoint. We were terrified, the both of us, leading each other further out.

We decided to move. Kurt couldn't stand to be in the city any more, and I wanted to get out of there as well, I didn't care where we went. One day I came home to find him suddenly delighted. His face, which had been dead for so long, had given way. His cousin in Nyborg was selling his late uncle's farm. We could set off to see it right away, make a picnic out of it. I remember it clearly, the first time I saw the farm, my belly weighing more heavily as we passed through all the little rooms of the house. Then the cousin showed us the barn. He threw the door wide open, glancing back at us as though we'd bought a ticket to a sideshow at a fair. Inside there was a certain kind of silence. Metal. Dry, compacted grass.

I've never told anybody this, but after we moved to Funen, I went to a women's group meeting in Odense. There'd been a poster in the local bakery for ages. Everyone was welcome. The only requirement was showing up. I'd had to refuse that poster many times. The mere thought of all those women in a room, I'd said to myself, was exhausting. Then one day I took the bus and went to Odense. I felt crushed under the weight of what I needed from them – it was so vast and confusing that I had to turn it into anger. They'd be snobs, I decided, they'd hate me. I burst into the room, which wasn't very big, or it felt like I did, although in reality I probably slunk over to a chair. When my turn came to introduce myself and share why I'd come, I said I was there because of my relationship. Then I couldn't do it, I broke off. I loved Kurt, I couldn't betray him. I apologised and left the meeting despite their protests.

Everything looks so simple when you're far away enough. But if you zoom in, if you examine the situation with your heart, you realise you know nothing at all. You can call it love, but that's not an answer. It only begs a new and more incalculable question. They stopped, Kurt's fits of rage. Suddenly it had been years since the last one. But they didn't take my fear and anger with them. I still felt humiliated. Now that the cause of my emotions was receding into the past, they grew almost harder to bear. They were disgraceful remnants, I was swollen with them. I was trapped. Stuck in the old life while the new one moved on.

Still, I stayed, and told myself there were many good practical reasons for staying, that somehow it was for Sofie. But honestly I think what kept me there was love. Love, although I don't know what it is, or why it's revered. The pain that courses through me when I think of leaving Kurt is that of breasts engorged with milk.

You should have seen him dance when we first met. He was so handsome. I don't know if he still dances, if anyone in

Nyborg does. I don't know any of those people he hangs around with, Bent, or any of the others. They kept on coming for a while, now and then, but eventually I chased them out. I was brutal. I told Kurt, whose face was open and afraid: Your whole life is a joke.

There is a delicacy to him. If there's anything I truly love him for, it's that. People always think it's something else you love them for. The other day, out of the blue, he promised me a house in Spain, and I couldn't understand what made him think I wanted that. No, it is his delicacy, his devotion so easily wounded, because it is unconditional. Like that swallow's nest, destroyed in the storm. Or all the litters of kittens we've had by now, and he's always as excited as ever, or as downcast when some don't survive the birth. I love that about him. He can't bear to see a dying potted plant. Not like me. I'm neglectful. I forget the things around me. Honestly, I never thought you could be jealous of a potted plant, but I have been, sometimes.

I can't bear to say much more right now. It's been hard enough already, and I don't think it helps. As I tell my story, there's a certain grimace of his, or a smile, I can't get out of my head. I first saw it one day when I said a few harsh words to Kurt. He was hungover. Exposed, exhausted – I think I knew he was vulnerable. Unusually for him, he had no unkind words in response. He looked up at me abruptly, with a face like a child's, and then a warped and momentary smile crossed his lips.

Maggie wakes up on the sofa. Almost three a.m. She folds down the corner of her thriller. There's a question at the back of her mind – must be the book that put it there. *Who did it?*

The flatness of the night outside the window. She is alone inside the dull and dazzling square that is the room.

# AT CAFÉ BLOMSTEN

It was before they'd moved, after she had decided to come back from Berlin. She got off at Friheden Station, no reason really, and followed a path up the hill. She sat down at the top and looked out across the water. It wasn't until she got up to leave that she saw the fox below her on the path, only a few yards away. It stood quite still, staring at her. Are you going to eat my belly? Aren't you frightened of me? You're so pretty, just don't eat my baby. That was the beginning. It must have been Sofie who drew in the animals. Whenever Maggie sat down, a heron arrived, or suddenly the footpath in the park was thick with frogs, and she didn't dare move forward or back for fear of treading on them. Once, after a fight with Kurt, she had gone off into the forest on her bike, pedalling hard all the way to Kongelunden. She told the belly-child they were going to pick flowers, but she sensed the baby probably knew better than she did that she was trying to cycle faster than the fear. She sat down on a tree stump. A squirrel darted right past her feet. What's the matter with you, she thought, when suddenly there was a wild fluttering all around her. Birds, flying out from the treetops all at once, and the branches where they'd been perched flicked back into the air with a sprinkling of leaves. Then she turned and saw the sheep.

Not far behind her, a dead sheep. She hurried off, but then changed her mind and walked back very slowly. She didn't know enough about sheep to tell if it was young or old. The sheep, which had once been living, was now dead.

Maggie has got lost in memories. It's as though, now Sofie has moved out, she has had to reassure herself she's still her mother, that she has the right to travel into town in that capacity to meet her. She's still on the bus, already heading out of town again, when it occurs to her she was supposed to get off. Shit, she blurts out loud, and now she's even more eager to get off, before everything starts trickling out of her.

On Nørregade in the town centre she's dreaming of a proper city. Shanghai, New York, Bangkok, Paris, Tehran, Cairo, Sao Paolo. In these cities there are pigeons in the squares, there is light and fluffy bread or pancakes, shrimp, a sweet and faintly giddying scent of petrol, crowding in the metro.

Maggie is imagining the scene. There would be gulls above the water. Examining the soundscape of the fantasy, what she hears are the shrieks of gulls, the iron chains of the boats as they bob against the harbour, taut then slackened, conversations murmured among the other patrons on the terrace at the harbour-side café. She pictures spring, early sun. A chill still carried on the wind. Sofie sitting across from Maggie, laughing, as though she knows the life Maggie has dreamed up. She knows the American sun, the Chinese sun; she knows the simple but delicious breakfast on her plate, the little plastic tub with something sweet and strange to smear onto the toast. All of those things she has been given by her mother, and she doesn't even realise it, because this Sofie doesn't know another mother is possible: a woman who, to spare her daughter from herself, receded into daydreams, into apathy.

Café Blomsten is on a little side street. There are wicker chairs outside it on the pavement. It's a real café, and not, as Maggie had assumed beforehand, a pub with a pretentious name. The sign is hand-painted. Red, with the name in big gold letters. They probably didn't mean for the o to be quite so far from the l. Head back, mouth agape, she soaks in everything about this gorgeous sign, until it strikes her that she must look odd, and she hurries to do something more normal, opening her bag and reaching in for her purse.

She dithers awkwardly in the middle of the café, before deciding in a rush of blood to act. Making herself as narrow as she can, she edges past a row of tight-packed tables and takes an empty seat in the big window overlooking the street.

Café Blomsten is heavily furnished. Faded green velour curtains, and a large mirror on the back wall in a frame carved extravagantly with flowers. Maggie gets the sense it's all supposed to suggest something, but she doesn't know what that is. A sense that meanings are doubled, with a message that is closed off to her. She wants to lift the dreams out of the room and into herself, the dreams her daughter has dreamed here, but she cannot reach them.

She starts to read the menu, otherwise she'll get too light-headed. All the dishes have French names. Quiche Lorraine. Croque Madame. She doesn't recognise the names, but she does know the ingredients in the descriptions. At first she thinks it's beautiful, abstract, like recognising your own neighbourhood on a map, but then she remembers that the names will have to be pronounced when she orders. She might have to ask Sofie, who actually speaks French, to do it.

In the old days Sofie was the one pointing determinedly at this or that, demanding to know the word for it. That's a screwdriver, a flower, a fridge, that's the sky, a chair; that's a chair, sweetheart, a chair.

In many ways, Sofie is living the dream Maggie had dreamed for her. She is going to university, she will earn her own money and won't need a man. But Maggie must have imagined the dream could be realised without her daughter becoming something too different from Maggie herself. Now she can't stop worrying that university is teaching Sofie something she herself senses only obscurely, that Sofie might open up a book and find her mother laid bare.

In her final year at home, Sofie was full of a sullen love that drove her, despite herself, to seek out Maggie in the kitchen in the mornings. She would take a seat on the bench, and they would smoke and drink coffee, talk or be silent, until one of them cycled to the bakery for breakfast rolls. With that they went their separate ways, and were apart until the following morning, when again, morose and drowsy, Sofie took her seat back on the bench, and let her mother work for her forgiveness. Now, though, that sullen face has been exchanged for a new one. Sofie's look is searching, tolerant, and Maggie quakes under her gaze.

You're cleverer than me, you won't come a cropper like I did, Maggie said recently to Sofie on the phone, and Sofie laughed and asked where had Maggie come up with that expression. Maggie had to hang up and find a dictionary to work out what cropper actually meant.

She'd heard the expression from her own mother, but after the conversation with Sofie she began to doubt herself. Maybe it wasn't cropper at all, but copper? Stopper? Then she couldn't help laughing either, although the truth was she was hurt. Hurt both that her mother's phrase was crumbling in her hands, unlikely ever to return, and that Sofie would rather tease her about the way she talks than listen to what she's actually trying to say.

The passers-by outside the glass are indistinct to Maggie, just a scattered stream of flapping anoraks and unknown errands, until suddenly one of them catches her eye. It's a woman in a burgundy coat, and there's something about the coat itself – and the haughty, fascinated smile – that makes Maggie think the woman has slept with Kurt. In a flash she remembers what it's like to slide down Kurt's cock, and is shocked by the desire that awakens in her body. She straightens in her chair, pelvis tensed, twisting to throttle back the memory.

In Nyborg especially, but even as far away as Odense, she wonders what people know and do not know about her. She has no friends, and nobody to talk to except Sofie, so if people do know things about her then they must have come from Kurt.

She has no doubt that she's a laughingstock. It's classic. The younger model ends up stultifying on the farm, growing just as old and silly as the ex. Strange to think she used to wonder what Kurt ever saw in Ulla. It's unlikely anybody knows that she was the one who asked him to find somebody else. She couldn't sleep with him again, not one single solitary time more. She asked him to find somebody else, and it was a relief, but temporary, like pushing long and hard and only letting out a brief and silent fart.

The door to Café Blomsten opens once again. This time, Maggie knows without having to turn around that it's her daughter. Something in the air that changes. A scent, an inimitable tempo.

So, Mum, what are you up to these days? Oh, says Maggie. There are the flowerbeds. The faltering project with the hedge. There was something wrong with the scissors. The scissors, she repeats, then pulls a face. You know what I mean – the shears, that's the one. And I didn't fancy telling your father. You know how he is, he'll start lecturing. How you fix them, what the little parts are called, and honestly I just don't care. But it's not like I could take them somewhere else to be repaired, either, oh no, that would be high treason. So I left it. Frankly, I'm quite happy having an excuse not to trim it. It really doesn't matter – where's the harm in letting it grow? I was looking forward to your father saying something so I could ask him: What *is* the harm. But apparently there isn't any. I don't think he's even noticed. So I suppose there wasn't any point, me trimming the hedge all these years. I certainly wasn't doing it on my own account, or the hedge's. Oh, I read some of that book you gave me, by the way. Freud. Felt a little overblown. You know, I was thinking – if Freud is supposed to be a genius, I was thinking what a genius I could have been, if only I'd had the time for it.

But suddenly Maggie thinks she's said too much. She was so pleased to see her daughter, words spinning out like whirlwinds, and when Sofie started laughing, Maggie took it as far as she could to keep the laughter going, but now it dies away, and Sofie's face is grave.

A child at the next table squirts ketchup onto his omelette, and a story she saw on the news pops into Maggie's head. The police, letting some American children out of a barn where they were being held. The children moving slowly, blinking in the sun. It's criminal, to film them at a time like that. They were clinging to each other underneath the open sky, a cluster of them. She gets the urge to tell Sofie about the children, but decides against it. Can they be comforted, she wants to ask, not just set free but comforted?

They sit in silence at Café Blomsten.

Then Maggie thinks to ask about university. Yeah, Sofie's got a really good lecturer at the moment. It's a class on psychoanalysis from a feminist perspective. As Sofie talks, she presses crumbs of pie onto her index finger and guides them from the plate onto a napkin, where she wipes them off. Maggie struggles not to laugh at this peculiar transfer. Then Sofie looks up from her plate. Mum, were you a feminist when you were young?

Maggie is embarrassed. She doesn't understand what Sofie's really asking. If this is an accusation. Then, a rush of anger. So Sofie's going to tell her, is she, how she should have lived her life? Sofie, who has no idea of what it is to go without something, who can read everything she needs to know about in books.

But Maggie knows her anger is unjustified. If Sofie doesn't know about her life, if that makes Maggie feel lonely and misunderstood, then she only has herself to blame. She's never really told Sofie anything about how she lived before Sofie was born. Or, for that matter, much about what happened next. If it ever came up, then it was only to serve as a warning.

It's so easy for things to escalate. To end up very wrong. That's what she's hinted to Sofie that she knows about. She has let this knowledge leak out in an enigmatic and not unintentionally terrifying way, acting on the notion that Sofie had to be protected from doing the same as she did, but without actually revealing what that was – perhaps she scarcely knows herself. She was trying to erase any traces of her own life in her daughter, she supposes, and ended up hurting them both.

\*

Sofie has resumed the transfer of the crumbs, and it occurs to Maggie that she isn't sure how much time has passed since Sofie asked the question. No, she says, but in a way that sounds more like a question than an answer.

The look that Sofie gives her now isn't the tolerant one. Or the searching one. There are no levels to it. She is looking at her mother from a sadness Maggie will never understand. Alright, well, why don't we try the juice, she asks, with that superior air she has of rescuing her mother out of her own deep waters, and Maggie smiles, relieved.

While Sofie gets up to order, Maggie's thoughts wander back to Rome. Oranges and those big beautiful silver machines the coffee comes out of. If she'd had Sofie in Rome, things might have been different. They might be sitting in a square in the sun, in secretive and vaguely frivolous conversation about things only they understand, because only they have lived their life. *Their* life, in a flat too cold in winter and too hot in summer, that is small and pretty and has a balcony Maggie will sometimes glance out at from the living room, and see that Sofie's out there, deep in thought.

Maggie is far off in the daydream when Sofie sets a juice down in front of her. In it is a stripy straw. There's a comical moment when they both look up from their straws at the same time and stare into each other's funny sucking faces. Probably they both needed to laugh, because Maggie ends up guffawing so hard that juice shoots out of her nose, and then Sofie bursts out laughing too.

*

But Mum, says Sofie, when they've calmed down, there's something I want to tell you. I'm seeing someone, and it's a girl.

Maggie looks in bewilderment at Sofie, who assumes of course it must be horror, anger written on her mother's face. But something else is welling up in Maggie.

Helpless, already resigned, Maggie had been waiting for the day she would have to stand there mute and stupid as a houseplant while she overheard Sofie's boyfriend calling her a whore behind the closed door of her bedroom.

She has had a few boys over in the past. Maggie opened the door to them and stared into their faces, but they were only mirrors leading back to her own life. She had no idea what to do about the devastation she thought would inevitably catch up with Sofie.

Kurt has wished Maggie dead, burned, run over, cancer-stricken. So what was she supposed to say when Sofie's boyfriend wished her dead, when some man made her daughter think she might be better off not living? Of course, Sofie would have to leave him. But how could Maggie say that with any authority?

Now, in blissful ignorance, she imagines all her fears have been unwarranted. That Sofie's been let off, that Maggie has too.

Maggie puts her hand on the table, palm upturned. Sofie doesn't accept the invitation at first – she's hurt by the look on Maggie's face. Then, tears running, Maggie says she loves Sofie, that she's proud of her, and Sofie takes her hand.

Maggie buys a bottle of champagne. It's awkward even as she first suggests it, and even more so when it's wheeled out in a big bucket of ice. Neither of them has seen it presented that way before. But then the bubbles make them light: it's as though they're both no more than feathers on the wind, each carried in their own direction when they part outside the café.

She's woozy with champagne and animation when she gets home. She can't help it – she tells Kurt, first making him promise he will never admit to Sofie that she let the cat out of the bag. Kurt needs a moment to recover. First, from the mere fact of this alliance between mother and daughter, which means he is never the first person Sofie comes to. Then because Sofie seems to be turning more and more towards a trusted and secret circle of women. But finally something else comes over him. A smile that swells. That loosens. Well Maggie, I'll be damned. Our daughter has her first girlfriend.

Maggie looks at the man she has spent her life with. The hands dangling restless at his sides, as though they had once been birds, before they were caught and recast into this low-hanging life. She pours a beer into two glasses, says, why don't they go and sit outside for a while?

# KURT'S LIFE REVIEWED

He can hear Maggie clattering with something in another room. Then she passes through the living room, carrying a piece of colourful furniture, a little bedside table. She's holding it so that the four legs poke out from her chest, making her look like some strange insect. They never did get married. That was the plan, at first – they dreamed the whole thing out together – then they forgot about it. Kurt's not sure which would have looked worse: getting married for the third time or having a baby with his girlfriend. If they'd got married, he thinks, it would have felt right calling Maggie his wife. Girlfriend, on the other hand, seems wrong. That's not his girlfriend, the woman walking through the living room like a colourful insect. Maybe it's because you can be estranged from your wife, but she's still your wife. Being estranged from your girlfriend is a contradiction in terms.

He lies down exhausted on the sofa. Above his head is a crayon drawing Sofie did years ago, a tiger floating in a blue sky. A floating sun, two floating palm trees and the floating tiger – such are the contents of that world.

He's eighteen, it's his first time in the long, eerie corridors of the maternity ward, waiting to see his wife. By the time he comes into the room, they have whisked the child away. Bodil needs rest, but it doesn't seem as though she's going to get any. He wants to take her hand, but she pulls it back and stares at him like he's a ghost.

A few months after the baby is born, on the night Bodil announces that she wants to leave them and then actually does, it doesn't feel real. Kurt listens by the door, expecting to hear her coming up the stairs at any moment, but she never comes back.

When the baby wakes up in the night and screams, he has no idea what to do. It flails in his hands when he picks it up, its head flops back, he has to grab it and lay it against his chest. Then the baby starts rooting for the nipple, and frantically he thinks of food he could give it. It's almost impossible to open the fridge door with the baby in his arms, so he puts it down carefully on the armchair, wincing because by now it's shaking with its sobs. They don't have any milk. Flummoxed, he opens all the kitchen cupboards without knowing what he's looking for, until finally he reaches in for a bottle of juice. The baby cries even harder when he tries to drip a suitable dose of the liquid into its mouth from a teaspoon. It's obviously not satisfied. Still pursued by its cries, he boils up the juice with some flour, waits impatiently for it to cool, then feeds it to the child. It helps. They fall asleep together in the armchair, the baby on Kurt's stomach, equally exhausted.

The next morning he has to go into work with the baby in his arms and resign. People silently make a path for him as he walks through the factory hall. The disgusted pity he can sense around him makes him feel like hurling the child to the ground, but he holds on, moving up the steps and to the door, into the office where he only recently signed his contract. On the way home he goes to the pharmacy, buys a bottle. Buttermilk diluted with water is best, says the pharmacist, who to Kurt's relief asks no questions.

After its milk, the child falls asleep in his arms. He places it cautiously onto the bed and lies down next to it. The baby's name is Flemming, but it probably hasn't got used to that yet, and neither has Kurt. He looks at the little face, the little mouth, from which a faint rattle emerges. Only now that the child is motherless does he truly grasp that it's alive, that there is a heart beating behind its ribs. He stays for a while and watches it sleep, at times incredulous, at times flooded by the pain that is love.

It's a clear, frosty morning when he breaks his last fifty at the supermarket. He walks home down Sankt Peders

Stræde with the buttermilk in his hand and his heart swelling for the little one it is his job to feed. He dreamed the other night that Flemming had teeth, but then they turned out to be rotten copper coins, rattling out of him as he broke into an eerie old-man's laugh. At home, Flemming is sucking his toes in the crib. Kurt looks down at his child, and it is unfathomable what he did to bring about this life. He picks up Flemming, holds him, and they pace back and forth through the two rooms of the flat while Kurt considers his options. He's heard that men pick up other men on Rådhuspladsen. That's his best solution. Flemming usually sleeps four hours at a stretch before he wakes up in the middle of the night, by which time Kurt will be home. Otherwise he'll have to put a bottle in the crib and hope Flemming can make use of it.

It's insult added to injury: Bodil's betrayal, and now wearing that betrayal on his body, regularly putting on a costume that's meant to be alluring. At night he paces back and forth across the square in a leather jacket and tight trousers. After a while, if nobody approaches him, he runs on home. Outside the door, he hesitates. He's afraid of finding Flemming dead inside, imagines reaching into the crib and placing a hand on Flemming's chest and discovering it isn't moving. But Flemming's only sleeping. It drives him mad not knowing if the baby cried for him while he was gone.

The sun is high, and Kurt goes down to the paddock. Sofie is still just a pudgy little ball rolling around in the yard, grazing her knees, revealing something deep and earthy every time she laughs. She came up to him the other day while he was lying on the grass, sat down on his belly and peed. You little beast, he said into her warm hair, almost overflowing with sun-dazed love.

Reaching the paddock, he kneels down in front of Turner and rests his head against her chest. Calmly she lets him do it, bending her head and nuzzling his cheek. She is his only confidante. He doesn't speak to her with words, he tells her everything by other means. Nobody but him can ride her. She's defiant if they try, bridling or refusing to walk at all. He apologises for his stubborn horse, secretly delighted by their pact.

Ib, their neighbour, had been on the verge of sending her to the knacker's yard. The horse was incorrigible. His daughters weren't getting any use out of her, in fact she snapped at them the minute they went near her with the currycomb. Kurt had walked past the horse in the paddock every day without feeling anything in particular. He thought it belonged where it was. But once he understood it wasn't wanted, once he saw in it the implacable, unbending love of life that Ib was so eager to kill, he offered the absurdly high sum required so that Ib – who wanted to punish the animal for not submitting to his daughters – would agree to move the horse into a new paddock next to the one where it had previously been kept.

Maggie stares after him oddly every time he goes down the path to Turner's paddock. He thinks about it with his cheek against the warm, smooth-coated ribs. If she's jealous. She's a funny one, the woman he dragged out here. Other people barely register with her. You introduce her to a friend and she holds out her hand, but you can tell they go straight through her without leaving a trace. Yet she is interested in his relationship with Turner. Her face is telling when he comes back from the paddock, but Kurt doesn't have the energy to puzzle out what it's saying. If Maggie doesn't get it, that's her business. Only in Turner's company can he think calmly.

An idea has started taking shape in him. He wants to make a clean break. Like the sun rising in the morning, unhesitant and measured, he will ascend out of the wage-earner's life. No more driving other people's buses. Every day he'll put a bit aside – he doesn't mind taking a second job, a night shift, if he has to – and eventually he'll have enough to buy an old bus and start out on his own. His thoughts flow out of him and into Turner. He can tell she wants him to be free as well.

Sofie calls with the news that Maggie is dead. She thinks Kurt ought to know that Maggie suffered, that it wasn't peaceful, if that's what he was thinking. He wasn't, but then again he hadn't thought anything much; he hadn't wanted to think about how death begins in a body that is still alive. He has always considered life and death two very different, disconnected things. For the most part he's avoided any thought at all about what was happening inside of Maggie. He had to imagine her like a peel with nothing in it. Now he rushes to the bathroom to throw up. It doesn't stop, even after he has nothing left to give. Standing bent over the sink, he sees that Maggie's brush is still on the shelf, full of hair. Unaccountable, that the hair no longer belongs to someone. He takes the brush and slides down against the wall, and he's still sitting like that when Sofie comes in hours later. He doesn't know what to say. He holds up the brush to her almost like a shield, and she twists it out of his hand and yanks him up. It looks like she's about to hit him, but then she slackens, slumps down on the toilet. For a while they sit in silence, then they help each other to the sofa. Kurt switches on the TV, where the presenter is bounding to and fro in a colourful shirt. Pain transported. From father and daughter to the television, and from the television back to them: as a brand-new shiny silver car, a shrieking audience.

Hvidovre, long ago. Kurt is a child, looking out at fields that never seem to end. Cows grazed here once, but now the land has been bought by the state. They're going to build a new road. It's midday, and the sun has turned its wrath on Kurt, but he has no intention of stopping, he'll keep walking till it's night.

Yesterday his father took him to the abattoir where he works. He walked straight in among the peeled cows hanging from the ceiling, a cigarette dangling from his mouth. But Kurt didn't want to follow, or no, he *couldn't* step inside the house of death, where he now realised his father worked, and he began to cry. A little way into the hall, his father turned and saw Kurt standing by the door in tears. For a moment he looked confused, then he began to laugh. Other men peered out from between the hanging corpses, more and more of them searching for the source of the merriment. They saw him in the doorway, and soon the whole hall rang with laughter.

So now Kurt is walking across the fields. He can't forgive his father, and if a person can't forgive their father, that person has no home. He tramples through the wiry grass, and as night falls he sits against a tree and cries because he's hungry. He looks up at the sky, which stares bluely back. One day he'll hang up all the adults, he promises someone who is neither himself nor a specific other. There is greatness coming, and he'll be the one who shares it out.

Kurt is sleeping badly, sweatily, in his office, the way he sleeps when he's been drinking, when Fatih prods his shoulder with a fingertip. It's an overstep for both of them, perhaps for Fatih especially, for whom the sight of his boss's bare legs is an unpleasant reminder of the chicken thighs he ate the day before. Maggie is screaming in the barn, that's what Fatih has come to tell him. Kurt pulls on his trousers and runs across the yard bare-chested. When he sees Maggie, he doesn't know what he's looking at. His first impulse is rage. Suspicion, the next. What does she want from him? That's all he can ask. He grabs her arm and drags her back into the house, sits her on the sofa. There's nothing behind her eyes, but he knows she's putting it on. Dragging his employees into this is an indignity he will not forgive. An old wave rolls through him – he hasn't felt it for a long time. His chest expands, pressure building in his temples; there is a rage in his hands that longs to shake her, but instead he tells her to die. Nobody will miss you, not even Sofie.

All day long she lies on the sofa. He keeps coming back to her: he wants to touch her, but he knows he's made that impossible. By nightfall she is so exhausted by her anger that she lets him crawl up next to her. I love you, he tells her, and she replies in the same way.

Insects swarm above the shallow water in Nyborg's moat. The smell of lilac is so strong it almost reeks of it in the square, where a family, worn out by the heat, are bent over their pizzas.

I have known since I saw the farm that the white-haired man was dying. He gave me what was left of himself, the better to make his escape. I think it's happening today. It will be a close, quiet death in his room at the nursing home.

He'll go to take a midday nap and fade away alone.

For now, he's in his chair. Not taking stock of his life, exactly, more like flipping absent-mindedly through the people he has lost.

The last time he saw Bent was at Jovan's funeral, not long after Maggie died. Another hard pew near another coffin. Dreadful.

The mood at the wake was fluttery, nervous. Most of them had only discovered after his death that Jovan had been diagnosed with AIDS. Nobody really knew what to say to anybody else across the tables. Gradually they clustered in small huddles, whispering about who had been with who, and how.

Bent and Kurt left and went to the Gull, a new place by the harbour that looked like all the old places.

They had a disagreement, something about money. Who, over the years, had reached for their wallet more often. Well, they made up. Neither of them really cared, as long as the other one didn't care either. The rest of the night went well. There was a tender gravity to their drunkenness, a humility, because they were still alive and had each other.

But in the months that followed, neither of them called. They got out of the habit of each other, until the thought of meeting up grew more and more onerous. They bumped into each other once or twice, but Kurt didn't go out much any more, and then Bent moved to Odense.

Kurt doesn't know when his own parents died, but they must be dead.

He's fallen out with all his siblings. Unlike him, they outgrew their anger towards their parents. It's easier to get on in life if you forget.

But Kurt can't forget, and anyway, he was the youngest child, making him the one his parents most regretted. It was him, more than the others, who made it impossible to make ends meet. Him, more than the others, who could have made all their lives easier by not being born.

He himself has brought three children into the world.

There's Flemming. Mette, who he had with Ulla. And Sofie, the only one he ever sees. And then only occasionally.

Flemming he had to take to a children's home. He coped for three years, but after that he couldn't do it to the boy any more. They were barely scraping by, and when they did eat, it often wasn't enough.

The home was in a big, red-brick building. A woman met them in the front hall, led them to the dormitory and to the bed where Flemming's name was written on a little blackboard. Kurt set down the rucksack at the foot of the bed, trying his best not to think about the fact that it was all he had to give to his son.

Hand in hand, he and Flemming followed the woman as she opened different doors, waved an arm and named the rooms. Back in the dormitory, Kurt held the boy in his arms. Flemming clung to him. Kurt cried, but silently, so Flemming wouldn't notice.

How was it possible to tear himself away from that embrace? He's asked himself a thousand times. Not in words, not directly, but as a rush of pain from within his chest and down his abdomen.

\*

He tore himself away, his insides screaming as he opened the door and nodded at the woman, who had gone to wait in the corridor. Yes, he and Flemming had said goodbye.

Outside the main entrance, he watched as the woman knelt and put her arm around Flemming's shoulders. They waved at Kurt, who barely made it out of the front garden and around the corner before he collapsed onto the pavement, vomiting into a hedge.

For many nights after that he woke up in a cold sweat, hearing Flemming scream. He reached out for him, to the place where his bed had been, and realised anew the boy was gone.

Less than a year went by, and he received a letter from the director of the children's home. There was a couple who wanted to adopt Flemming. They were good people, wrote the director: he was a priest and she a teacher. They lived in Rungsted and kept a wonderful garden. A better home, the letter concluded, was hard to imagine.

That last sentence was particularly tyrannical. Wasn't the best home imaginable the one Kurt could have given Flemming if he'd had the money?

But Kurt had no defence. He cried, writing a response to say how delighted he was to receive the director's letter.

Mette, he has no idea what happened to her.

\*

She became Ulla's child when he left.

Every six months, via a friend, he sent them an envelope containing as much money as he could spare, which Ulla, according to the friend, always opened angrily.

On the rare occasions when he went to Copenhagen, he avoided all eye contact with girls he thought must be around Mette's age.

In any case, Maggie was becoming increasingly bitter about anything that reminded her of his previous marriage. He didn't want to bring up Mette, get her mixed up in that bitterness.

Sofie, too, is slipping through his fingers.

He never quite gets around to calling.

He can't wrap his mind around the idea of making calculations several weeks in advance and scheduling a time to meet in Copenhagen, where she lives; that he can't just drop in. Time has grown different for them. His is unbroken, no longer parcelled out in words, while hers – *how about the first week in September, Saturday*, she might ask, and Kurt doesn't know what she means, or whether he'll be dead by then.

Sometimes, Sofie calls him.

He sits in the wicker chair in the hall, the one next to the residents' phone, and is made uneasy by the listeners, mute presences in other wicker chairs in earshot. Knitting, staring.

He has nothing to say on the phone. Him, the man who used to talk and talk, who'd start running his mouth the minute he got out of bed in the morning: he has nothing to say now into this stupid tube.

He glances down the hall. There are fourteen rooms. Names beside the doors, on whiteboards from which the name can easily be wiped and replaced with another.

You should get a mobile phone, Sofie says to him.

He could tell her he hates those buttonless screens. That it frightens him the way you can't open them up and inspect the mechanics of them, that no one, in his opinion, should cede so much control, but he only answers, mm, yes well, perhaps he should.

He's mourned so long he isn't sure these days that's even what he's doing. It's become a habit, but a habit he can't shake, because the truth is, he is in mourning.

It was Maggie's death that brought the whole thing down about his ears. Flemming started screaming again in Kurt's dreams, and soon he was doing it by day as well. Kurt shut himself inside his bedroom, trying to shake the tears out of his head.

\*

He'd been held in place by Maggie's condemnation, just about. With her gaze no longer resting on him, pinning him down, there were no borders any more. He fell apart.

Not long after her death came the bankruptcy. The bank owned him, right down to his underwear. They were entitled to everything he had. He was forced to leave the farm.

For many years he lived in a small flat in Nyborg.

He made an agreement with the supermarket to have his shopping delivered, which made it largely unnecessary to go out.

When the outside world did obtrude, it was mostly in the form of windowed envelopes. He left the letters on the coffee table and didn't open them. Now and then, eyes averted, he swept them all into a bag, tied it hastily closed and threw it out.

The money he used to have laughed at him from the television, which he did still have. At the time when he bought it, it was the most expensive model in the shop.

Then they cut off the electricity. It wasn't until Sofie turned up unannounced one night, knocking on the door, and Kurt answered wearing a head torch and led her into the unlit flat, that she decided from then on his post should be redirected to her.

*

It was Sofie who insisted he be put into a home.

It's a violation, really, living in a place like this, where he feels at any moment someone might come barging in and catch him in the act of something. Life in here is a series of arrangements – him in the armchair with his feet up, him in bed, him with knife and fork in hand – which are designed to prevent anybody finding out what he really wants, although even he doesn't know what that is.

When he moved in he brought nothing but a single box. He refused to explain its contents to anybody. They're relics. A spoon Maggie left on the kitchen counter the morning she went into hospital. A little make-up bag he has rarely opened, for fear of letting something out and losing it. But he knows the smell of the lipsticks, an inexplicable scent, bluish. There is nothing else that smells like that.

He put Sofie's tiger drawing in the box as well, and hung it on the wall above the bed. He likes to dream that he's the tiger, free-floating among the palms. When Sofie comes for one of her rare visits, it's a thing he often does. He points to the drawing and says: You made that. I really like it.

And now he's going to die.

I'm not sure he notices, because he's sleeping. His chest stills, his breathing stops.

Sofie arrives a few hours later. She finds it in herself to stroke her dead father's hair. Standing there, her mind is blank. If anything, it is a sea, an endlessness of translucent molluscs.

Then she exchanges a few words with a nurse. About what came before, about the death, how it happened, and a little more about the practicalities at hand, where her father will be moved, and how long he can stay there.

Something plunges through her, streaming out in her wake as she shuts the door and leaves her father on the bed.

# A CALL FROM
COPENHAGEN

Before we end, for now, I want to tell you about a night that Kurt at first remembered only vaguely. He'd been out with Bent. First at the Phoenix, then they moved on to the Cadet. Lene had been there too, dangling off Kurt's neck until she gave up and went home, feeling like she'd degraded herself for a man she didn't even really like. She fell asleep with the light on, exposed, as she felt, to a gaze from which she was too exhausted to shield herself. Kurt, meanwhile, was only getting started. The world around him was a merry lurching blur – he talked louder and louder, reeling off ideas as quickly as he drank, more and more of them whisking him away. He woke the next morning with something at the back of his mind, but couldn't pinpoint what it was. Then, a few days later, he received a phone call from a man who introduced himself as T.

Great time the other night, said T, his voice both jovial and jeering, and it had the intended effect on Kurt, who felt instantly dominated. Nice place, Nyborg, but I didn't know you lot had money to burn. T said he'd been in the transportation business for some years now. He'd spotted a great opportunity, a project. The idea was to break the state monopoly on shipping across the strait between Zealand and Funen: a simple matter, as he put it, of taking over a couple of ferries and doing it more cheaply. There's no better investment for your money right now. Kurt grew frantic, flushed; it sounded like a venture that could take him further than he'd ever dared to dream. But he didn't want to seem like he had no other options, so he said to T he had to think it over, and hung up. For the next few hours he paced his office, jittery, euphoric with vengeance. He thought about all the people who wanted to see him fail, all the people for whom his life was an indifferent, little life. Those were the people he was answering when, a few hours later, he could wait no longer. He called T up and said they had a deal.

# SCANDINAVIAN STAR

~~Part One – Money to Burn~~
Part Two – The Devil Book
Part Three – Maria, Atlantis
Part Four – Ideas 2
Part Five – Jørgen Is Sacrificed
Part Six – Silence
Part Seven – Watertown

penguin.co.uk/vintage